MARGARET CARR

BLOOD WILL OUT

Complete and Unabridged

LINFORD
Leicester

First published in Great Britain in 1975

First Linford Mystery Edition
published July 1988

British Library CIP Data

Carr, Margaret
Blood will out.—Large print ed.—
Linford mystery library
I. Title
823′.914[F]

ISBN 0-7089-6564-4

Published by
F. A. Thorpe (Publishing) Ltd.
Anstey, Leicestershire
Set by Rowland Phototypesetting Ltd.
Bury St. Edmunds, Suffolk
Printed and bound in Great Britain by
T. J. Press (Padstow) Ltd., Padstow, Cornwall

1

THE daffodils around the narrow grave bobbed and danced in the brisk March wind and I finished weeding out the last of the speared green grass which had thrust its way between the trumpeting ranks and sat back on my heels. My mother lay there, at peace at last.

She had wanted to be cremated, her ashes scattered over the banks of the river, among the wildflowers she had loved so much, but my stepfather hadn't allowed that. It wasn't his way.

I stared with loathing at the multiplicity of angels on the headstone. That was his way; the vulgar, the ostentatious, the pretentious. The sanctimonious sentimentality of the text sickened me. A hypocrite too.

Six red roses lay at the foot of the grave. He made a ceremony of his grief once a week, choosing his moment when everyone attending morning service could bear witness to his sorrowing devotion.

A slow walk to the grave, the solemn moment of offering, the bowed head, the silent prayer, the heavy tread into church where he would sit through the service, his cherubic face shining with piety and true christian spirit.

He was a good man. Most people thought so—if they didn't have too many close dealings with him. After three months of living in the same house I was beginning to know the meaning of the word hate. What was worse was the thought of how my mother must have felt. She had been married to him for ten years and she was far more vulnerable than I.

A widow with a ten year old child; a widow driving herself to an early grave in her efforts to give her child the advantages she felt compelled to provide.

My father had been an officer in the Royal Air Force. An officer and a gentleman! How often had I heard that phrase from her, said with such pride. It was no use telling my mother that the two weren't necessarily synominous. She was fixed in her beliefs, single minded in her efforts. I had to have ballet lessons, piano lessons, elocution lessons. I couldn't play with the other children in the neighbourhood. I had to work hard at school and be top of the class.

Inevitably I'd rebelled. What child wants to be set apart from his fellows? What child likes to be different, to be called names and held up to ridicule? I'd tried so hard to be one of them that I went to the other extreme.

I think my mother married Ken Manning in despair. She thought she was never going to make it on her own. At ten years old I was one of the rowdiest little hoydens ever.

I was sent away to school before their marriage and when I returned for the holidays my home was no longer in one of the little terraced houses in the valley. We had moved to the hill, to the residential area where the mill owners had built their homes in the booming days when cotton was king and Carsdale, a thriving town, when the chimneys had poured forth their smoke, the town had been run to the sound of the hooter, the mill workers hurried to and from work, their clogged feet clattering on the cobbles.

The cobbles had nearly all gone these days, and most of the mills, rows of the terraced houses lay derelict waiting for the final death blow but there was still some prestige in living

3

on the hill. It was becoming a retreat for the richer people from Manchester, able to afford the time and money to commute. Ken Manning worked in Manchester. I never had known what his job was and I didn't want to know. It provided him with a great deal of money. That much was evident. My mother had everything she could ever want. People said how good he was to her—and to me. We were both considered to be very lucky. There was no working in the factory for my mother, doing other people's cleaning, working in a bar at night, addressing envelopes, sewing or doing the hundred and one things she tried in an attempt to earn money to provide for me. She had it made.

Two years after her marriage Chrissie was born. She was a miniature of my mother, golden-haired and blue-eyed. I adored her and I think it was through Chrissie I came to know my mother so much better. Or maybe I was at last settling down to being a human being. People called me names at school but this time it wasn't the little lady. Rather the reverse. My values were turned upside down and I had started to learn, finding out that enjoyed it.

I had no especial feelings for Ken Manning

then. He was just a man, a rather chubby little man with a face like an angelic cherub and baby blue eyes. He didn't like children very much and when I was home I didn't see much of him.

As I grew older I even felt rather sorry for him. My mother couldn't love him, not after she had loved my father.

It wasn't possible, rather like comparing the court jester with the handsome prince charming. For my father had been an outstandingly handsome man. My mother said I took after him but although it was true enough that I was dark as he was I thought the likeness was wishful thinking on her part. She had so few memories, so little to remind her of him.

The one tale she loved to tell had been of their meeting. A midsummer ball, the moon at its zenith, an encounter on the terrace, the scent of roses and honeysuckle and a dance under the stars in the flagged garden. She made it sound like a fairy tale.

She had been only eighteen. They were married a month later. It was 1941. A time of war, when marriage was rushed, honeymoons were brief and the waiting went on for ever. He never came back. He was shot down over

Germany, never even knowing he had a daughter.

I hoped she was with him now. That was what she had wanted. She had died with his name on her lips and her hand in mine. I was in my second year at Oxford. He could be proud of me. She had made me what she thought he would want.

I was glad she couldn't see me now. My Oxford days were over. Ken had seen to that. He thought it stupid nonsense. A girl didn't need a university education. She learned other things that were more useful. I was to keep house, take my mother's place, look after him and Chrissie. I hadn't fought for my freedom. How could I? He made me feel I was deeply in his debt. How was I to guess that my mother had paid every day of her life with him for everything I had received? But I guessed that now. Those cherubic features hid a mind as cruel and devious as Satan. He held me prisoner with Chrissie as hostage—and he used her with me as he must have me with my mother.

A shadow fell across the grave and I glanced up and saw the vicar coming towards me.

He was an old man, his skin as soft and wrinkled as a last year's apple, his limbs stiff

6

and clumsy, his back bowed. He moved slowly and with care but his voice could still roar from the pulpit and his eyes light up with fervour. They were gentle now, as was his voice, filled with understanding and kindness.

"She loved the spring," he said looking down at the grave.

"Yes." I rose to my feet, dusting the earth from my hands. I would have liked to pick up the roses and fling them in the litter bin but Ken would know it was me and it would be Chrissie who would pay for it.

"I've not seen you at church lately," the vicar said. There was no accusation in his tone, only concern.

"No." I wasn't going to tell him that I couldn't bear to sit beside Ken. The vicar was a good man. A really good man. He wouldn't understand.

I had known him ever since I could remember. Religion didn't play a big part in my mother's life. She simply believed in God and paid her respects every Sunday, and she had brought me up the same way. I had strayed away from those good habits since I left school but not often, not until now, and I salved my conscience by taking the Sunday school class for the eight year olds, the one Chrissie was in. It had finished half an hour before and I had sent her on home to start the tea Ken insisted on having promptly at five on Sundays.

The vicar fell into step with me as I walked slowly out of the churchyard. "You don't blame anyone for your mother's death, do you?" he asked hesitantly.

I thought he meant I was blaming the Almighty and then I knew better. He saw beyond the mask with which people hid their inner thoughts, he could sense despair and turbulence, but he was incapable of seeing evil. I knew he wouldn't understand. My mother hadn't reached her fortieth year when she died. She had been cheated out of life. I hadn't blamed Ken at Christmas time but now I knew him so much better I knew why my mother had preferred to slip away without a fight.

"I'll tell you something," I said in a hard voice. "I'm glad she's dead. She's well out of it."

"Yes, she had a hard life," the vicar said reflectively. "But you brought her great joy. Always remember that. It will comfort you. And her last years were easier."

"Were they?" I said bitterly, unable to hold that back.

"Your father tells me you're not returning to Oxford." The vicar decided it would be wiser to change the subject.

"*Step*father." He wasn't my father. He never could be. The one thing my mother had held out against was an official adoption and the changing of my name. Terence Howard wouldn't have wanted that. I was his daughter and no one else would lay claim on me. Ken hadn't liked it. He still didn't. He felt it would give him more power over me if I were adopted.

The vicar blinked and then said mildly, "He's been very good to you, Elinor."

"So he constantly reminds me but he didn't have any choice in the matter—not if he wanted to marry my mother."

"Did your mother tell you that?" The vicar sounded shocked.

"She didn't have to. I know the kind of man he is and I know my mother. She married him for my sake. She didn't love him."

"That's a very sweeping statement to make. Love comes in many different forms. You're loyal to your own father, Elinor. You hate to feel that anyone could ever have taken his place.

9

Do you not think you are allowing this feeling to stand in the way of achieving a good relationship with your stepfather?" He was severe now. I wasn't being a good Christian.

I shook my head. It wasn't worth arguing about it. It had been silly of me to say anything at all. Ken's position was impregnable here in Carsdale. He had worked too hard at his image.

I ran home, slipping in by the back gate. I was late but Chrissie was laying the table for tea, her face intent and serious. I brought out the salad I'd prepared and added the plates, checking that she had placed the knives and forks in the right place and that everything was in order. Ken was at his best when he caught me out. The lady was ignorant. She didn't know her right from her left. He had picked on the name which had plagued my childhood and used it constantly.

He came swooping out of his den just as I was filling the teapot and he glanced pointedly at his watch and said, "You're late."

I was allowed half an hour after Chrissie got home. No more.

"I was talking to the vicar," I said levelly.

"Oh? What did he have to say?"

"He said you'd told him I wasn't going back to Oxford."

"And he wanted to know why? Did you tell him then? Did the tears come into your eyes as you told your sad tale? She doesn't want to look after you, Chrissie, my dear. She'd sooner you went into a home so that she can go back to her student friends. Little girls are no company for the lady here."

Chrissie stiffened as if she'd been struck. Ken kept undermining the relationship I tried so hard to build up, his little pinpricks adding to her feeling of insecurity. She stared at me, blinking hard and said in a wobbly voice, "That's not true, is it, Nell?"

"Of course it isn't. One little girl is very good company indeed, especially when she is just like you." I smiled at her reassuringly, wishing I could make her believe I would never leave her, that I loved her. She had been very quiet since my mother's death, prone to bouts of weeping. I kept trying to make her laugh again. If my mother had done it under odds like these I should be able to at least win a smile now and then, but it was uphill going. She had been with my mother the most of course. She was bound to miss her more. But the young were resilient.

11

It was Easter soon. I had planned to take her out a bit. There was the Sunday school outing too. That was something for her to look forward to.

We sat down and I said brightly, "Guess where we're going on Easter Saturday. Out for the whole day on a coach. We shall see some lovely gardens and a great big house where they have old-fashioned cars and carriages and lots of things you've never seen before."

A flash of interest brightened Chrissie's eyes but Ken said, "What's this then?" He stabbed at a pickled onion and gnawed on it making sucking noises. He turned my stomach.

"The annual outing for the children. We're going to Tatton Park."

"Oh? Just like that? What about me? No thought of asking for my permission?" He sat lolling back in his chair, his baby blue eyes alight with malice. He enjoyed spoiling things. Bringing tears gave him immense pleasure. Anger, frustration and disappointment were emotions that fed his ego. Fear was the most satisfying of all. I was learning to keep a tight rein in his presence. He would never know how much it cost me.

I said evenly, "If you feel I shouldn't go,

perhaps you would make my excuses to the vicar. As one of the Sunday school teachers he expects me to do my share of looking after the children."

I had him there. His eyes hardened and he gave me a long measuring look. I wasn't beaten yet. There were other ways of hitting back, maybe not quite as exhilarating as open defiance but more successful. He couldn't be certain that I had deliberately picked on the one thing where he was vulnerable. His self esteem wouldn't allow that he had a weak link in his armour.

"You can go," he said with an air of doing me a favour. "Only see that you make proper arrangements for my meals. You can get someone in. That Mrs. Singer from the pub. She wouldn't mind obliging and while she's here she can give the place a spring-clean. There's nothing but dust and grime since your mother died. You've got a lot to learn about cleaning."

I didn't deny that. He was exaggerating of course. I did my best. But it wasn't like my mother's handiwork. She had only to flick a duster and the furniture had shone. Or so it had seemed. She must have worked every minute of the day in actual fact. It was a big house.

Chrissie relaxed at his words. No opposition. "Where's Tatton Park?"

"Out in the country, darling. In Cheshire. They have a Japanese garden and a lake and lots and lots of flowers."

"What kind of flowers?" She was like my mother with her passion for the things of nature.

I did my best from memory. I had been once. My mother had taken me when I was younger, about the same age as Chrissie. I remembered the big Tenants' Hall filled with the most unusual things brought by the late Lord Egerton from his travels abroad. They had fascinated me much more than the house. That had been boring to a little girl and I couldn't imagine that anyone had actually lived there. I still couldn't imagine it, seeing it for the second time. We trooped around, gazing earnestly at the big heavy paintings, the solid furniture and the big sombre rooms. The children preferred the gardens as I had done; the Orangery, the New Zealand Fernery and, of course, the Japanese gardens and the little

14

bridge, the mere with its moorhens gliding smoothly across the water.

We had taken a picnic lunch to eat in the grounds. It had turned out to be a fine day, always a worry when planning outings for children, and at three o'clock the vicar announced that he had a special treat in store for us. We were to have tea at Winters Hall.

The news was received blankly. No one had heard of the place. The vicar looked around, faltered a little and then rallied, telling us gently that it was one of Cheshire's oldest homes and had only recently been opened for public viewing.

It was presently owned and occupied by the de Howard family who had been in possession for the last two hundred years. The building largely dated from the second half of the fifteenth century but there had been constant additions and renovations and it presented a somewhat hotch potch view with its different roof levels, jutting gables and tall chimney stacks, the black and white herringbone much in evidence on the front elevation, with its tall casement windows glittering in the sunshine.

We piled out of the coach and trooped up to the elegant white door. No massive oaken portals here. There was a bell and a letter box and it was like going into an ordinary home except for the suits of armour standing in the corners of the hall.

A woman stood before a little table where stacks of brochures were displayed. She came forward to meet the vicar who explained who we were.

"Ah, yes. The group from Carsdale, and you must be Mr. Walton." She shook hands. "I am Beryl Howard. My daughter is waiting to be your guide."

She opened a door in the panelling behind her and we had a glimpse of a comfortably furnished room as she called out, "Madeleine," and then a girl strolled through standing to regard us with slightly amused eyes.

She had black hair hanging loose down her back and her eyes looked black as well, with lashes like the thick curling fans of a Japanese doll. Her cheekbones were high and flat, her nose straight with slightly flaring nostrils. She wore trousers and a high-collared shirt with a scarf at her throat. She looked casual and at ease, and yet she was at home in the grand surroundings, not like her mother whose studied elegance was artificial and out of place, an overplaying of the part of mistress of Winters Hall for the benefit of the gaping sightseers who were too ignorant to recognize quality unless it was dressed up for them.

I didn't like Beryl Howard. I took immediate exception to the condescension in her tone as she spoke to the vicar and handed him one of the brochures. Her eyes were hard and her lips thin. She had slimmed to the point of skeletal angularity and her hair was touched up to a pale unconvincing gold set in apparently casual waves.

She asked the vicar to be sure that none of the children ducked under the guide ropes or touched anything, her tone making it very obvious that she had doubts about letting children in wholesale.

"We don't usually cater for groups so young," she informed him. "After all, they don't appreciate what they see."

The vicar assured her earnestly that she would have no cause to worry and Madeleine took over, smiling brilliantly at him. "I'm sure that children who go to Sunday school must be paragons of virtue. If you'll come this way I'll show you over the house and then we'll have tea. We've set a table out on the north lawn as it's such a beautiful day. This is the library.

We were allowed about a foot inside the room before the guide rope stretched across the length of it stopped us from treading further.

The ceiling was low and ridged with heavy black beams. Books lined three of the walls completely from floor to ceiling, big dark volumes that looked as if they had never been opened for centuries. A fireplace took up most of the fourth wall; a Tudor fireplace Madeleine informed us, pointing out the intricacies of the carving above. The windows were at either side, sash windows inserted about the beginning of the eighteenth century.

"The Morrisons owned this house and the land for miles around," Madeleine remarked. She didn't sound as if she were reciting from a memorized piece but rather as if she was enjoying telling the history of the house. "They were Catholics and Royalists and landed themselves into trouble with both Elizabeth and Cromwell, so the house has all the essential features of secret passages and priests' holes." She had the attention of all the children right away with such a statement.

18

"Can we see them?" one of them piped up eagerly, his face aglow.

Madeleine laughed and assured him they could see one of the priests' holes. "There were two," she said. One had been discovered only five years ago when the central heating system was installed.

"And the passages?"

"No," she said regretfully. It was too dangerous. They hadn't been used for years and years. But she told them when they had been used. She had a gift with children. There were no dry facts and figures which would have soon started them fidgeting, but bloodstirring stories of cavaliers and roundheads, feuds and duels, escapes and capture, a beheading, an elopement. And the curse which had been laid on the family for all time.

She paused as she started to tell us about this.

We had been going through the dining-room and then the drawing-room where she had been matching the tales to the portraits of all the long dead Morrisons and their ladies, and she had stopped before a dark sombre portrait of a young man. The paint was cracked and the picture looked about ready to fall apart. "We think this is the man who laid the curse," she said. "It was found in the priest's hole I was just telling you about and as you can see it's not in very good condition. We think it was hidden for when the time came for Jasper Morrison to claim Winters Hall as his own. He was the son of Henry Morrison." She moved to another portrait showing a man with long curled hair and a strong ruthless face. "Henry was a friend of Charles II and inevitably he fell foul of the dissolute life at court at that time. He was wildly extravagent and the most reckless of men. Many of his lands and estates were sold off to pay his debts and when he broke his back in a hunting accident he retired to Winters Hall. He was still a comparatively rich man however and when he died a cousin moved in to claim everything as his. Henry had never married and Jasper was illegitimate. He was turned out of the home he had considered would be his." She glanced back at the portrait of Jasper. "Maybe if he had been older he'd have fought. The story goes that he was only seventeen. He cursed the Morrison who turned him out and swore that tragedy would always haunt the man who sat in his place. He also took the King's favour, a ruby given to Henry by Charles. There it is on his finger. It was supposed to be lucky for anyone to hold a gift of the King's. He made sure they had nothing to counteract his curse. And of course it was very valuable."

We all dutifully stared at Henry. The ring was on his little finger, a great stone extending to the knuckle. "It never turned up again," Madeleine said. "Neither did Jasper."

"And did the curse work?" Betty Singer asked. She was the daughter of the Mrs. Singer Ken had termed obliging. The same couldn't be said of Betty, a pudding faced girl with a bird brain but a certain vicious animal cunning that gave her a hold over what she termed her friends. I had been at school with her before I was sent away and the antipathy between us was mutual.

Madeleine didn't answer for a moment and then she said soberly, "Yes. The cousin lost everything but Winters Hall and he died of a particularly virulent disease that ate his flesh away. The last of the Morrisons died over two hundred years ago and from what we can make out every one who inherited suffered some kind of tragedy that ruined his life and made it a mockery of living. Even afterwards . . ." She moved along to another portrait. "Christian de Howard. The first of the Howards at Winters

Hall. He laughed at tales of the curse. He was a hard man. He'd made his money through the slave traffic and he'd been cursed before, many times. He had a daughter, a beautiful girl whom he worshipped. She disappeared in the first summer they were installed and he spent the rest of his life looking for her. It turned his brain in the end. This is her portrait. Her name was Anna."

She was very like Madeleine; the same high cheekbones and slanting eyes, the wide mouth with its hint of sensuality and passion allied with a kind of reckless generosity.

"I think she ran away," Madeleine said thoughtfully. "I think she fell in love with someone she knew her father would destroy. He would never have let her go. This is his son. He never lived at the Hall and he appears to have lived to a ripe old age without anything blighting his life. Whether he believed in the curse is not a matter of record but he certainly didn't take any chances. *His* son was another matter. It was almost as if missing a generation had increased the potency of the curse. His wife was a . . ." She caught herself up, recalling that it was a party of children she was addressing, "A . . . a bad woman," she substituted smoothly. "And he was a proud man. She made his life a torment for many years until at last something broke in him and he shut her up in one of the turret rooms. No one ever saw her again until the day she died. He alone saw to her needs. It wasn't for very long. She killed herself after less than a year of her solitary confinement. I'll show you the room where she was put. He died not long after her. Strangely enough people said it was of a broken heart."

"And what happened to the next owner?" Betty asked. She had taken a dislike to Madeleine. I'd suffered too often in the past to fail to recognize the signs. She was poised ready for the ridiculing witticism that would bring the titters from her audience, an expression hovering between pseudo respect and anticipated gratification on her face. "You're not really trying to tell us you believe in a curse? You look intelligent enough."

Madeleine regarded her coolly, with not even a flicker of her lashes to show she was disconcerted by such rudeness, and for the first time I saw the reason for Betty's antagonism. I had never attempted to analyse it when it was directed at myself and indeed, I couldn't see why she should feel it of me, but of Madeleine it was obvious. Betty was envious. Envious of all the things Madeleine represented; power, money, privilege. Envious of the way she looked, the natural authority that had held us all spellbound. With every aid available Betty could never be like Madeleine. And she knew it, and so sought to destroy or drag down to her own level—as she had dragged me down, so often and with such success. But Madeleine wasn't like me.

"I believe in it," she said softly. "Only the blind can ignore the evidence put right before their eyes. Scoff if you like. The ignorant usually do. This is the next owner. He was my great grandfather. A fine man, wouldn't you say? But he died in a leper colony with half his face eaten away. His wife contracted the disease on a visit to India and he looked after her until she died."

Betty had gone a brilliant red. She opened her mouth and then shut it again without uttering a word. There was nothing she could say to that.

Madeleine smiled at her. "You don't die quickly from leprosy," she said gently and she turned around and mounted a curving flight of stairs which came out in a long gallery where even more paintings were hung. There were not so many portraits; Turner and Constable predominated.

I hung back, herding up the last of the children who were inclined to lag behind but once they were in front of me I paused, disturbed by a sense of familiarity. It was almost as if I had been here before. I took a few steps forward.

It was a trick of the brain; one part working a split second out of gear to make it seem a repetition of something that had happened instead of what was happening at the present time. I'd heard it explained by other people, and how could it seem familiar when the ground floor of the house had awakened no reverberations. How?

I put out my hand. I *knew* a little pressure would make part of the panelling swing around as if on a pivot. I stepped through without a moment's hesitation and before the panelling swung back on me saw the shelves of sheets and towels. And then it was dark. Down below a little daylight lightened the bottom of some steep stairs and fell across a stone flagged floor.

They would lead to the kitchen. No secret passage this but the linen cupboard and the servants' stairs. A discreet route for the maids to whisk away the chamber pots and replenish the fires, to change the beds and carry out all the menial duties the gentry would find distasteful to see.

There would be a light but I didn't need it. The stairs went on and though my brain told me that they were bound to go on up to what had been the servants' attic quarters the pulling sense of familiarity told me that there would be no dusty, cramped quarters left vacant from the days when these houses had an army of indoor servants. I hesitated, the scent of lavender in my nostrils, but the pull was too strong. I went on up. I knew just how many stairs there would be and stopped on the top one without taking a false step, pushing against the door which barred the way. It swung open at a touch.

One more step and I was inside. I stood quite still. It was what I had expected and yet it was different. I didn't know how or in what way. It was a large room with black beams arching high in the exposed roof in a crazy criss-cross of acute angles across white plaster. The windows were small and leaded and allowed in little light but there was enough to see that the room had been furnished with great care. It was all a whole, a completely harmonious picture of comfort, beauty and peace. Above all peace. Impossible to imagine that voices were ever raised here, that hate and unhappiness existed. My eyes were drawn to the piano. The lid was open. It was there—an invitation—as the whole room was an invitation, drawing me forward, embracing me in a cloud of welcome that was a spell of enchantment. I went slowly across the pale green Chinese carpet and sat down on the piano stool.

Ken had sold our piano only two weeks after my mother's death. He said my playing disturbed him but I knew very well that if I had taken no pleasure from playing, it would have remained there as a mute example of his culture. Not many people in Carsdale had a piano.

I ran my fingers lightly over the keys. I had no sense of doing anything wrong, of being where I had no right to be. I had forgotten about the children, even Chrissie. Beethoven, to match this room, this feeling of peace. Sedate and lovely.

The music rippled from my fingers and I was lost, playing better than I had ever played before.

Until a strangled cough cut right through my

27

absorption and made me stop abruptly. The spell was broken. I was appalled at what I had done.

I rose to my feet apprehensively, my eyes darting round the room. The cough was repeated, a harsh tearing sound that pin-pointed itself from a high winged chair turned away from me.

I wanted nothing more than to flee but a voice followed the cough as if sensing my desire. "Don't go. That was a fool thing to do. I was enjoying that." He was breathless, the coughing had racked his lungs. And then he took a deep breath and his voice steadied, "I'd like to hear some more."

"I didn't know anyone was here," I faltered. As if that was an excuse for the really unpardonable thing I had done.

"I gathered that." I thought I detected amusement. "For your sins, play on."

I didn't have any choice. Not really.

Beethoven was gone, the mood banished. The Sorcerer's Apprentice, the sense of sinning, the flurry and panic. I felt it all.

When I'd finished and the last chord faded into silence he said. "You play well." This time there was no doubt about the amusement. He added, "How did you slip by Beryl's vigilant eye?"

"I found the linen cupboard."

"Oh?" There was a movement, at once suppressed, as if he'd intended to lean forward to look at me. "How did you spot that?"

"I don't know. I put out my hand and there it was." I stood up awkwardly. "I'd better go. They'll be looking for me." Glancing at my watch I could hardly believe it. Over an hour had gone by. "Thank you for not telling me off. I'm not usually so rude."

"Wait a minute." He paused and then said slowly, "Don't you have a piano of your own?"

"Not now."

"You may come again if you wish."

I was disconcerted and couldn't think what to say. I wished I could see him. It was eerie talking to a disembodied voice. "How kind you are. First by not throwing me out and then extending such an invitation. I wish I could accept but my home is in Carsdale and it's a long way to come."

"Well, if you do pass this way again you know how to get here. I have very few visitors. You'd be very welcome."

Visitors! As if he were an invalid . . . Perhaps

he was paralysed in some way. But there had
been that movement . . .

"Thank you," I murmured and I turned to
the door. It didn't move at my touch and I
hesitated for a moment and then almost of their
own volition my fingers went to a knothole
hidden low down on the door. They slid in
snugly and I could pull the door open.

Behind me I heard a quick intake of breath.
The man half whispered, "Who are you?"

"My name is Elinor Howard. I'm—" I half
turned and was frozen into complete immo-
bility. He was standing in very much the same
frozen stillness in which I stared at him. But he
had no face, or not a face as I knew it. It was
like a rough hewn sculpture with the features
barely delineated; deep pits for eyes, a blob of
a nose, a gash for a mouth and the skin the
pitted stone, scored and ridged with the white-
ness of death.

The tale Madeleine had told about her great
grandfather leapt to my mind. The leprosy
eating away at his face. I didn't stop to think
that this could be no ghost. I fled like a terrified
rabbit as his sudden upflung arm broke the spell
that held me transfixed. I must have touched
the stairs, I couldn't have jumped over the

whole lot, but I had no memory of how I got away and I tumbled out into the gallery without a thought for anyone who might deservedly be startled at the sudden materialization of a white faced girl from out of the panelling.

Fortunately the gallery was empty. I gave no one a heart attack.

I sped in the direction Madeleine had taken. The gallery came out into a complex of bedrooms leading into one another. Only one had a fourposter, the other beds were modern divans with silk covers and discreetly placed controls for electric blankets. I slowed behind a party of four. There was no room to pass. The ropes allowed only a narrow passage through the bedrooms with a length of stair carpet protecting the pale beige fitted carpet which ran right through the bedrooms. There was central heating, slender white radiators in every room, and bathrooms, pink, blue and yellow suites in what must have been the dressing-rooms at one time.

We came out of the bedrooms at another staircase, a wide, beautifully proportioned flight in magnificent dark oak; the main staircase, with shallow steps to allow the crinolined ladies to descend without hindrance.

The group in front of me paused to look at the portrait placed at the head of the stairs and I slipped past them. No more portraits for me. I wanted to get out, out into the fresh air. The enforced slowing down of the headlong flight had brought a return of common sense. It wasn't a ghost. Only a man . . . a man with a face he knew would bring horror to anyone seeing him. No wonder he had stayed behind the sheltering cover of his chair. Was that how he lived? Hidden away where no one could see him?

My steps faltered. I turned back. I had to see him again. I couldn't leave him thinking he had frightened me off like a Frankenstein monster. Slowly and reluctantly I mounted the stairs again. I didn't want to go back but somehow I felt I owed it to him.

The group passed me on the stairs and the portrait was straight in front of me; a dark handsome man in the uniform of the Royal Air Force.

I stood stock still staring in disbelief.

That was my father up there. Or if it wasn't he had a twin who had posed for the photograph which had been my mother's most treasured possession for so many years.

2

A SECOND shock within the hour was too much for my system. A sickly wave of coldness moved swiftly over my body, enveloping me in numbness. It wasn't real. I was imagining things. I closed my eyes but when I opened them again the portrait was just the same. It was my father. I couldn't have been mistaken. I mounted the rest of the stairs, dragging myself up with an effort that was almost a pain. The plaque at the bottom of the portrait was black on gold. Inex Domincaro was the painter. And the sitter was George Terence Edward Howard, painted in 1938 in his twenty-fifth year.

And in 1941 he had married my mother. In his 28th year. Or had he?

I could feel myself swaying but there was nothing I could do about it and then there was a long, long blackness and I opened my eyes and Madeleine was bending over me with Mr. Walton hovering in the background.

I was lying down on something hard. The floor, at the bottom of the stairs.

Mr. Walton cried, "My dear child! What happened? Are you all right?"

I felt anything but all right. I closed my eyes again without answering and heard Madeleine's voice, worried and uncertain. "I don't think any bones are broken, but perhaps I ought to send for the doctor."

And then a hurricane latched itself on to me, frantic fingers pawing at my shoulder, salty tears splashing down on to my face, a warm body close to mine.

"Nell! Nell!" It was Chrissie, shaking me hysterically. "What's the matter? Why are you lying down like this? Open your eyes."

"Come away, Christine," Mr. Walton said firmly, and the frantic fingers were pulled from my shoulder.

"She looks—she looks like mother." There was such anguish in Chrissie's voice that it brought me sharply back from the numbing mists into which I was losing myself and I said faintly, "Don't worry, Chrissie. I'm not dead yet." My voice sounded so far away I barely heard it myself. I had to do better than that.

"Drink this," Madeleine said firmly.

It was brandy. I choked on it at first and then swallowed greedily. It made me feel better. I felt strength returning to my weakened limbs. I was aware of her arm supporting me. She smelt of flowers, a blend of spring and summer blooms.

"I hurt," I said, feeling surprise at the extent of it. My legs, my arms, my head as I struggled up into a sitting position.

"You fell down the stairs," a strange voice interposed. I opened my eyes. It was one of the women who had been in the group ahead of me. She had a plump round face with bright eyes. "You gave us such a shock. Standing there one minute staring at the picture and then suddenly crumpling up. There was nothing we could do. We were at the bottom."

"I'm sorry I frightened you." I managed to stand up. With so many pairs of eyes on me it was a command performance but the smile was for Chrissie. She was huddled against Mr. Walton, shivering like a frightened puppy. "I'm all right, Chrissie. It was just a little accident. Nothing to worry about. Now where's my shoe?" I had lost it somewhere and Chrissie retrieved it, still not reassured but happier now that I was on my feet. I cupped her face in my

35

hands. "I'm all right," I repeated. "Don't be such a little goose. Now run along and join your friends."

"Are you coming too?"

"Yes. In a moment."

"We had just finished tea," Mr. Walton said, "when it was realized you were missing."

"I'd love a cup of tea," I said quickly. "Do you think there will be any left?" I didn't want any questions. I didn't want to explain where I had been or why I had fainted. I didn't want to think about it. Not until I was by myself somewhere.

Madeleine. Could she be related to me? A half sister perhaps? Was that her father's portrait at the head of the stairs? I wanted to ask but I couldn't bring myself to do it.

"Thank you for the brandy," I said.

"There's more if you want it," she said. "And frankly I think you could do with it."

"No, a cup of tea is all I want."

"Right ho." She took my arm casually but I could feel the strength of the support she was giving me and was ashamed because I was glad of it.

The tea was in a huge urn and there was

plenty left. Most of the children had settled for orange juice.

Mr. Walton got it for me and piled in the sugar, no doubt as a remedy for shock. I was glad of that too. I felt as weak as a kitten.

Madeleine pulled up a chair for me and went off with the brandy glass in her hand. I guessed she was going for a refill despite my protest.

We were on a sunken lawn, square in shape, and a long table had been placed in the centre of it. The children eyed me curiously, whispering amongst themselves. Chrissie was watching me and I straightened my slumping shoulders and tried to act naturally.

Betty was watching me too but I wasn't aware of it until she said, "Where did you get to then? We thought you'd invited yourself to tea with your fancy relations. Too good to stay with us, of course. Always thinking yourself the lady."

I stared at her blankly and she raised her eyebrows, glancing around to invite others to share in the joke. "Didn't you tell them your name was Howard too and your father was an officer and a gentleman. I can't believe you'd miss such an opportunity."

The years rolled back. I was at school, the victim of her familiar taunts. But this time it was so much worse because it could be true. I retaliated as I had retaliated then, with violence.

The vicar seized my arm. "Elinor!" he cried in a shocked voice.

I stared at the knife I had clenched in my hand and with a shudder let it drop back on the table. I would have hurt her given the chance. I knew it. Betty knew it too. She had flinched away, alarm in her eyes, but at Mr. Walton's intervention she laughed, hitting out to pay me back for having frightened her. "I think I struck a sensitive spot there. Maybe she thought she'd do just that. Or maybe she was trying to find herself a place in the family tree and the shock of finding out she was just a nobody was too much for her."

The vicar turned on her sternly. "We'll have no more of such talk, Betty. Elinor had an accident."

"Ah, but what caused it? She's not the fainting sort."

"There are hundreds and thousands of Howards in the country," I said in a voice that sounded most unlike my own. "Pick up any telephone directory and you'll see them. Pages and pages of them."

"Yes, yes, of course," the vicar agreed,

looking harassed and worried. "Perhaps we should have sent for the doctor after all."

"No. I'm all right," I said sharply. I wouldn't allow Betty's baiting to affect me any more.

"Here," Madeleine said, and tipped another brandy into my tea. I wondered how long she'd been standing there.

"When did you drop the 'de' from your name, Madeleine?" Betty asked in an oily, ingratiating voice that grated on my ears. Even the vicar winced and I thought for a moment that Madeleine wasn't going to answer. The look she turned on Betty would have frozen a boiling kettle in mid-stream. "Round about the time of the First World War as a matter of fact. Why do you ask?"

"Did you have any black sheep noted for their promiscuity?"

That was too much for Mr. Walton. "Betty!" he said sharply. "That will be quite enough. Go and round up the children. It's time we started for home."

"But surely it's a possibility that—"

The fire flashed, the bowed back straightened. She knew when it was wiser to stop but as she moved away she couldn't resist one parting shot. "I thought the lady would want to know. She's held her head up high so long on her pretensions."

I sipped the tea. The rush of heat to my body after feeling so cold made me feel giddy.

"What did she mean?" Madeleine said in a puzzled voice, staring after Betty.

"Nothing," I said shortly. "She likes to upset people." She couldn't have guessed. She couldn't possibly. But that photograph hadn't been hidden away, not until my mother had married Ken. Would Betty have remembered it from when she was a child? No, of course she wouldn't. It was just her usual malicious talk. She couldn't know how closely she had struck home.

"What *did* make you faint?"

"I don't know." I put down the teacup. "Thank you for your concern and the brandy. I'm afraid I've put you to a lot of inconvenience."

"Wednesdays and Saturdays are days for inconvenience and upsets. We're getting used to it."

"What made you decide to open your home to the public?"

"Money," Madeleine said frankly. "What else? It costs a small fortune to keep up a place like this. My mother decided to jump on the band wagon. Why not? Everyone is doing it these days. She didn't think she'd lose face."

"Your father?" I choked. The words were difficult to get out. "Is he still alive?"

"No." Madeleine regarded me curiously. "He was killed in the war."

"Did he . . . ? Was he—?" It was no use. I couldn't get it out. Whatever I said it could be regarded as if I were trying to push myself on them for one reason or another—Betty's taunts were fresh in my mind. And did I want to know? Wouldn't it be better to forget this afternoon altogether? I spent a near sleepless night thinking about it. Impossible to forget. As soon as Ken had gone off to church I went into his bedroom. If my mother had been married she would have kept the marriage certificate. And my birth certificate . . . That had to be somewhere.

There was nothing in the drawers that had been my mother's. I opened the wardrobe but there was nothing there either. Ken had given all her clothes to the vicar to dispose of as he saw fit. I knew that. But there had to be other things she had kept. My school reports. She had been proud of those . . . the later ones that

41

is. And her jewellery. What had Ken done with that?

The den. Forbidden territory for me. I wasn't allowed in even to clean it.

I glanced at my watch. I had time . . . just. If I could find a way in. No. Better not to risk it. I could wait until tomorrow. I started the lunch instead.

It wasn't one of my more successful efforts. The beef didn't turn out the way Ken liked it, the gravy was watery, the roast potatoes crisped to such a hardness that Ken's first attempt to cut through one sent it skidding across his plate.

He put down his knife and fork in disgust. "You'll have to do better than this, my lady. What d'you call that?"

He pointed a finger at the Yorkshire pudding. It was flat and soggy. "It's a pity your mother didn't give you some lessons in cookery," he went on, "instead of all that foolish nonsense she wasted good money on. What use are your piano and ballet lessons to you now? I had a superb meal yesterday. Mrs. Singer could teach you a lot."

"I'm sure she could," I said meekly.

Ken regarded me suspiciously. "She could and she shall. I'll arrange it."

My heart sank. I chewed slowly on a piece of beef. Fatal to protest, it would only make him all the more determined.

"Well?" Ken demanded. "What have you to say about that?"

"You must do as you think best, of course." I raised my eyes. "But won't it cost you something? Mrs. Singer won't expect to do it for nothing."

"I think we can come to terms." There was a smirk on Ken's face. So he had enjoyed himself yesterday. I could well imagine it. Betty's mother had been a widow for a long time. She'd see Ken as quite a catch.

"I'll see her tonight," he said decidedly. "Now get me something else to eat. I can't eat rubbish like this."

I got up without a word and took one of the chops I'd got for tomorrow out of the fridge. Grilled, with instant mash and frozen peas, it didn't take long.

Chrissie had manfully struggled through half her dinner. I took the plates away and taking a long hard look at the apple pie decided it better not to risk another explosion and opened a tin of fruit with some cream instead.

Ken, of course, guessed what had happened and I didn't escape from comment. It was a relief to get out to Sunday school and afterwards I went to see the vicar and asked him if he still had the brochure Mrs. Howard had given to him.

"Yes, I still have it." He regarded me gravely. "What did happen yesterday, Elinor? The truth please. No excuses. I know you better than that."

I shook my head. "I'd sooner not tell you, Mr. Walton."

"It's not so very hard to guess. Betty hit on the truth, didn't she? You think you are related in some way to that family."

"And it seems impossible to you—as it would to anyone else. Mr. Walton, that was my father in that portrait at the head of the stairs."

"How can you be so sure?" He didn't sound surprised. I think he'd been expecting it.

"My mother had a photograph of him in uniform. It's the same man, I'd swear."

"And what do you intend to do about it?"

"I just want to know. I'm not going to barge

in there claiming relationship, if that's what you think."

"I don't think you'd do anything like that, Elinor, but I think perhaps it would be better if you let it drop, right now. You may stir up something that could be painful."

"You mean my mother might not have been married. I've already thought of that, Mr. Walton, but you knew my mother. Do you think it likely she would have claimed a marriage that didn't exist?"

"Your mother would have done anything for your sake."

"No. I don't believe it. She was married—or she thought she was. She wouldn't have lived a lie."

"Elinor, please. Be guided by me. Drop it."

I regarded him narrowly. There was something he wasn't telling me. "What is it?"

He turned away, pacing the floor.

I watched him in silence for a few minutes and then said, "You'd better tell me, Mr. Walton. I intend to write up to Somerset House if I can't find the marriage certificate at home."

He wheeled round slowly. "Your mother had no money but what she earned, Elinor. Why didn't she get the widow's pension?"

I could feel my face tightening. "She wouldn't have claimed it. You know how she felt about National Assistance and things like that."

"Your father was killed in the war. She was entitled to a pension from the War Office—that's not National Assistance."

"She would have thought of it in the same way."

He shook his head. "No, Elinor. I don't think she would. And she needed money desperately at times."

"I don't believe it. I don't believe it for one moment."

He was silent.

I said desperately, "She wouldn't have fought Ken when he wanted to adopt me. It would have all been covered up then."

"Perhaps she didn't want your stepfather to find out."

"But if I'm illegitimate and not entitled to the name Howard it would be bound to come out sooner or later. It would be on my birth certificate."

"Have you ever seen your birth certificate?"

"No. I started to look for it this morning

but I don't know what Ken has done with my mother's things."

"Find it first. Before you do anything else."

He really thought my mother capable of living a lie for all those years. I stared at him numbly.

"Elinor," he reached out and touched my shoulder gently, "don't you see that she would have done it for the best. It's not a crime."

"What do you know about the Howards? Why did you choose to go there?"

"There was an article in the Manchester *Evening News* about it. I only know what I've read and what we learned yesterday."

"The man in the portrait—is he Madeleine's father?"

"I don't know. The children were getting restless, wanting their tea. She didn't stop on the stairs."

"Could I have the brochure?"

"You'll find nothing in it of any help to you."

"You've already looked, haven't you?"

"I wondered, naturally—after what happened yesterday. Elinor . . ." He sighed. "I don't want to see you get hurt. It's easy enough to guess what happened. It was war time. People take chances when they know their life expectancy is low. Your mother came here after the war, to a place where no one knew her. She never talked about where she came from, she cut herself off completely from the past."

"And there had to be a reason . . . ? But it didn't have to be that reason. No!"

"All right, Elinor. I'll get the brochure for you." He gave up the attempt to persuade me to drop it but it was with reluctance that he handed over the little book. The pages were glossy, the pictures superb; the north wing, the south, the front elevation, the courtyard, the gardens, views of the individual rooms. I had missed a lot.

The pictures were detailed one after the other but there was no more information on that of my father's different from that on the plaque. He wasn't mentioned anywhere else either. There was a brief history of the house, mention of some of the Morrisons, a few of the Howards, but mainly the text was on the structure of the different parts of the building, the particular features of each room, the furniture and of course the paintings.

"You see?" the vicar said.

I nodded. "But may I keep it?"

"I don't think that wise. Sooner or later you

are going to think, I could be living there, that could be my home. Envy and resentment are corruptive emotions. Even if—" He broke off, shaking his head. "Come and talk to me again when you find your birth certificate."

"It will be perfectly in order. I know it will." I held tight to the brochure. "May I borrow it to read through properly, just once. I'll bring it back tomorrow I promise. That won't be long enough to corrupt me, will it?"

His face softened and he smiled. "Take it. I shouldn't have said that. You haven't an envious bone in your body."

Maybe he thought so but I wasn't so sure when I looked at the photographs. It was the kind of house that one dreams of owning the day all fairy tales come true. I was reading it in the safety and seclusion of my bed when I heard Ken come in.

He stumbled on the stairs and I heard him curse. He'd had too much to drink. Naturally enough, after an evening with Mrs. Singer. She didn't work behind a bar for nothing.

I glanced at the clock. After midnight. So she'd taken him home. Well, good luck to her. At least she'd kept him out of my hair.

I turned a page and then jumped as the door

was thumped open. He stood on the threshold, swaying a little. "We've been talking about you," he said. "You didn't tell me that you caused quite a commotion yesterday."

"I didn't think you'd be interested," I said flatly.

"I've heard all about it."

"I wouldn't believe all Betty says. She's inclined to romance. I fell down some stairs and fainted, that's all."

"And took a knife to Betty when she made a casual remark that was meant as a joke?"

Astonishingly I'd completely forgotten about that incident. I lowered my eyes and Ken laughed. "I knew you had a temper but it's a shock to find you'd go to such extremes. I think I'd better keep all the knives under lock and key. You might be tempted to use one on me."

"On my good, kind stepfather who gives me so much? No, surely not."

An ugly expression crossed his face. "You watch your tongue. I won't be spoken to like that."

"I'm sorry," I said wearily and with truth. It was stupid to provoke him. "It's late and I'm tired. I'm going to sleep." I reached out to switch the bed lamp off but he immediately snapped on the main light. "I've not finished with you. Mrs. Singer is coming round on Tuesday. I don't want any trouble. You'll do exactly as she tells you."

"Yes."

"And don't be cheeky to her."

"No."

He stepped forward, holding on to the end of the bed for support. "You're not like your mother."

I didn't know quite how to take that.

"She had her faults, but she knew how to keep on the right side of me. You've got a lot to learn yet."

I stared at him, afraid to answer back but willing to let him see the hate in my heart.

He said, "What's that book you're reading?"

"Nothing much." I slid it under the pillow. A mistake. He lurched forward once more. "Let's have it. Let's see what keeps you up so late reading in secret."

He probably thought it was a dirty book. It was the way his mind worked. I held it up, I had no intention of wrestling with him for it. "It belongs to the vicar. It's only something on the place we visited yesterday."

"Let's see it."

I handed it to him and he turned the pages, frowning over the print. "So you borrowed it?" he said. "The place impressed you so much?"

"I found it interesting."

"Really?" He smiled. "I'll have a read. You were going to sleep anyway."

"I have to return it tomorrow."

"Don't worry. I'm not going to run away with it."

I watched him go uneasily and then had to get out of bed because of course he had deliberately omitted to turn the light off. What else had Betty told him? If he guessed . . . I had to find that photograph. Tomorrow would be no use. I had forgotten it was a holiday and Ken would be home. And Tuesday, with Mrs. Singer around . . . It had to be now.

I gave Ken half an hour to settle down and then crept downstairs. I'd never tried to pick a lock before and not surprisingly had no success. I tried a knife against it, trying to force it back but that didn't work either. It would have to be the keys.

I crept back upstairs again and listened outside his door. He was snoring.

Cautiously I slipped through into his room, groping my way to the dressing-table.

He'd emptied his pockets. I could feel his wallet, the chink of loose change and then my fingers touched the coldness of steel.

There were almost a dozen keys on the ring. I wondered why on earth he had so many. The car, the house, his office, the den. What were all the others for?

Once in the den I found the reason for three more of them. There was a steel cabinet against the wall, a desk with every drawer locked and a safe set in a recess on a concrete base, a huge solid looking job that looked as if it would take dynamite to open without the key.

I circled around, careful not to make a sound. The room must have been intended for a small sitting-room when the house was built. It was pleasantly proportioned with a window over-looking the back garden, and although the desk and cabinet made it look like an office Ken had made it very comfortable for himself. There was a big electric fire, an immense armchair, a deep piled rug over the carpet. A bottle of scotch was on a low table by the chair, a thick book placed beside it. A legal book. I flipped over the pages. I'd never seen Ken reading anything like this. What on earth did he want with it? And all this security . . .

My stomach was already churning at the temerity of my actions. I turned to the door and locked myself in, suddenly convinced that if Ken found me here I'd be in deeper trouble than I had ever sampled from him before. If he should come downstairs I was going out by the window.

I went to the safe and found the right key. The obvious place for my mother's jewellery was there. And he might have placed her other things with it.

The door was heavy to pull open and the interior of the safe much smaller than it appeared from the outside. Even so there was still a lot of room and half of it was filled completely with stacks of bank notes.

Minutes must have gone by as I stared. They weren't brand new notes. I picked up one of the bundles. Pound notes, used, but in good condition.

How many of them? Hundreds? Thousands? I tried to estimate and gave up. I was feeling more and more edgy. There were a couple of box files in the bottom of the safe and I spotted the flat leather case my mother had kept her jewellery in. Ken had been generous. He liked her to wear his gifts, even though she didn't care much for most of what he gave her. He went for the gaudy and brilliant, regardless of design. It had to be conspicuous, for people to notice.

The box files were full of papers but there was nothing that looked as if it might belong to my mother. There were certainly no certificates there.

I opened the cabinet next and pulled open the top drawer. There were files inside, neatly named in alphabetical order. I pulled one out at random and turned the few pages. It seemed to be a detailed life history. I put it back. The second drawer was a continuation of the names, the third held a collection of tapes. Nothing of interest to me.

I went to the desk. The first drawer I opened had a gun lying on top.

I'd slammed it shut again before I realized what I was doing and the sound seemed to echo through the house.

I froze, straining my ears, until I realized that if I did hear a sound it would be then too late to do anything about getting away. I was scared, I didn't want to look any further. It was far simpler to write to Somerset House.

I switched off the light and opened the door

a crack. The house was in darkness. Maybe the sound hadn't been as loud as it seemed to me. And then a torch stabbed down like a miniature searchlight.

The door was locked again and I was through the window in less time than it took to blink. I dropped on to the ground and then couldn't reach up to pull the window down.

I left it. By then I was absolutely jittery with nerves. It seemed imperative that Ken shouldn't know I had been in the den, and what was worse, knew what was in the safe.

All that money . . . It had to be a tax fiddle. But that didn't explain the gun.

It was some consolation that I had his keys and he couldn't get at it to use on me. But I had to get back into the house and in my own room before Ken thought of looking for me.

I wasn't thinking very coherently. I picked up a rock from my mother's rockery and heaved it straight through the dining-room window.

The crash sounded like an explosion. I expected lights, some kind of commotion, Ken rushing out to see what had caused the noise, but nothing happened. And after the crash the silence was absolute. It was as if not only me but everything else was holding its breath.

A light went on but it was from next door. A minute later Mr. Jennings, a burly ex-policeman appeared. He walked around the windows of his own house and then stepped over the low dividing wall between the two gardens.

I crouched down behind a gratifyingly thick laurel bush, anticipating the loud knock he gave on the front door. Ken would have to come out now.

He answered the knock without switching on the hall light.

Mr. Jennings said succinctly, "I think someone's heaved a brick through your window, Mr. Manning. Didn't you hear the crash?"

Ken's reply was undistinguishable. He came out and viewed the damage with Mr. Jennings and then they both went inside and at last the lights came on.

I slid through the door and hovered in the hallway. I could have made it to the stairs but supposing they came out and caught me going up instead of down?

I went straight to the dining-room instead.

Ken was flat against the wall, Mr. Jennings in the act of picking up the stone.

My astonishment wasn't completely feigned as I stared at Ken. He was hugging the wall as if he were afraid of something. As if afraid that someone out there would take a potshot at him. I suddenly knew why he hadn't put the lights on. He wasn't going to make a target of himself.

"Whatever's the matter?" I cried. "Mr. Jennings! Oh! The window!" I stared at it in what I hoped was horrified surprise.

Maybe I overdid it. Ken's eyes narrowed and he regarded me coldly.

"We'd better get the police," I declared. "Or have you done it already?"

Ken's reaction wasn't entirely unexpected. After all he could hardly want the police poking in his affairs with what he had in the den.

"It's too late for that," he said. "Whoever it was will be miles away by now."

"Maybe . . . maybe not. In any case, you'll have to tell the police." I had a momentary qualm as I thought of fingerprints. Hadn't I read somewhere that rock wouldn't yield any help in that department? But maybe their techniques had improved. "I'll do it, shall I?"

I moved to the phone. The ring of keys in my hand burned like a branding iron. I don't know what I would have done if Ken hadn't stopped me before I could make any attempt at dialling. He could move swiftly when he wanted to for all that he was so fat.

"Go back to bed," he said curtly. "I'll handle this."

I went without argument. He'd acted predictably and I couldn't wait to get that ring of keys out of my possession and back where they belonged.

It was only when I was in bed that I thought he might have looked for his keys as an instinctive reaction when he got out of bed.

I should have dropped them on the floor. It was possible he could have knocked them off the dressing-table, *not* possible that they could have reappeared without my help. I worried about that for quite a while and then wondered why on earth I was getting so het up about it. What could he do to me? And then the more I thought about that the more apprehensive I felt. I didn't want to consider what he might do. There were depths to Ken about which I obviously knew nothing. And what I knew was bad enough.

3

I WAS late down the next morning, which was hardly surprising after two almost sleepless nights.

I threw the bacon in the pan and managed to set the table before Ken got down but that wasn't good enough for him. He wanted his breakfast on the table the moment he sat down.

I interrupted his sour comments abruptly asking him what the police had said. "Or didn't you phone them," I added as he stared at me blankly.

Maybe it was something in the way I said it. His pouting cupid lips tightened and for a moment I looked into eyes as cold and hard as frozen steel. In that moment I was frightened again. I felt the fluttering nerves start up in my stomach and churn away as they had done the night before.

But it was daylight now, the sun was shining. It was ridiculous to be frightened. He was a silly little man, hugging the wall like that, hiding in the darkness, afraid of making himself a target. Who would want to kill him?

I smiled at him. "I think they should know if someone is trying to kill you. That's what you thought, isn't it? That's what—"

"Shut up," he said, and although he didn't raise his voice there was such menace in it that I hurried back into the kitchen and decided not to say another word.

He watched me during breakfast. It made the bacon and egg taste rather like rancid curd and whey.

He couldn't have guessed. He couldn't.

Chrissie went off when she'd finished her milk. Apparently she and Libby Jennings from next door were going on a picnic again. It was only as far as the bottom of the garden but they were good at pretending. I gave them some biscuits to wrap up and after I had cleared away the breakfast dishes asked Ken for the brochure so that I could return it to the vicar. He mumbled something that I didn't catch and then said he didn't know where it was. "Tell him you lost it," he said carelessly.

"I'll do no such thing."

"It's probably in the bedroom then. Go and take a look."

I had an extreme reluctance to go into that bedroom again but it was the only way I'd get the brochure back. Ken wouldn't go up on my account.

But there was no sign of it. I looked by the bed and under the pillow, glancing around the room.

He'd left his keys out on the dressing-table, exactly where I had placed them last night.

I stared at them. He'd never done that before, not once.

And then a flicker in the mirror caught my eye and I saw him watching me. He knew. Not a guess. Not now. And he had sent me up here deliberately to see what my reaction would be. And like a fool I had shown my consternation.

I lifted my eyes slowly and met his in the mirror. I had seen Ken in many different guises but he rarely lost the basic cherubic foundation even at his nastiest.

It was there—the cupid bow, the chubby cheeks, the baby blue eyes—the heaven-sent props which were such a boon in fostering his image.

I had never imagined those pouting lips could flatten and disappear altogether, or that the cheeks could harden and tauten so that I could see the bone beneath the flesh and be reminded of a grinning skeleton, teeth exposed, humourless, merciless, without pity.

I could feel the colour ebbing from my cheeks and I tore my eyes away, my hands plucking nervously at nothing.

"I can't find it," I said loudly. "I can't find it anywhere."

"Have you tried in the den?"

"The den?" I tried to simulate surprise and was horrified at the tremor in my voice. "But it's locked. You told me to keep out of there."

"So I did. And you wouldn't dream of letting your curiosity get the better of you?"

"Of course not. Why should I?"

"Why should you indeed?" He nodded, not expecting an answer, and there were a few seconds tense stillness between us. Then he smiled. "There's your pamphlet." He had been holding it behind his back. "Have dinner ready for seven and see that you get that window fixed up. Oh . . ." He flung the brochure down on the bed and crossed to the dressing-table to pick up his keys. "I'd better not leave these lying around. Curiosity has a habit of killing the cat. Or didn't you know?"

It was a long time before I could bring myself

to move and then I had to shake myself out of the apprehension that held me fixed. He was my stepfather. What *could* he do to me?

I looked in on Chrissie before I went to the vicarage. Mr. Jennings was in the garden doing some planting and she and Libby had abandoned their picnic in favour of helping him.

He straightened up as he saw me and asked if everything was all right.

"My stepfather doesn't seem to be worried," I said flatly. "He just told me to get the window fixed. On a bank holiday! He expects miracles."

Mr. Jennings smiled. "I think I can help you there. I know someone in the business. Would you like me to fix it up? If not today I'm sure he could be there first thing in the morning."

"That's very kind of you. I'd appreciate it."

"He didn't phone the police then?"

"No."

Mr. Jennings shook his head. "That's silly. Maybe they can't do anything but it's surprising what the sight of a police car cruising around can do. They wouldn't try again. I think I'll call myself. Next time it might be my window."

"Yes, well . . ." I got away from Mr. Jennings as soon as I could. He liked to talk of

64

the time when he'd been in the force and it got a little monotonous with constant repetition.

The vicar was just coming out of the church as I passed and he called me over, the worry lines around his eyes deepening as he studied my face.

"I didn't ask you yesterday how you were," he said. "It was quite a fall."

"Only bumps and bruises," I assured him.

"I had a caller this morning. He was asking about you. He said he was Madeleine's brother and she had been worried about you . . . and as he was passing . . ." He let it trail off and then he said abruptly, "He wanted to know where you lived."

"And you told him?"

Yes, he had told him. And regretted it almost right away. Had he done the right thing?

"It can't do any harm," I said cheerfully.

"You realize it was just an excuse. They must have been curious about you."

"Did you manage to ask any questions yourself?"

"I'm sorry, Elinor. He caught me at a bad time. I didn't think. It was only afterwards . . ." He wasn't happy, not at all. He said abruptly, "Did you find your birth certificate?"

"No. I'll write up for a copy this afternoon."

"There was something about that young man I didn't take to. Elinor, don't do anything on impulse." He jerked his head as his house-keeper called his name from the side door of the vicarage. He was wanted on the phone.

"I'll see you again," he said. "Remember. Be careful."

It was an odd thing for the vicar to say. Odder still for him to come right out and give a warning about someone. In his world people were never bad, merely misguided. And why tell me to be careful?

I went home thoughtfully. Ken's instruction about dinner implied that he would be out all day. I wondered where. On a bank holiday he wouldn't be going to work. I made lunch for Chrissie and myself and afterwards took her and Libby down to the recreation ground. Mr. Jennings said he would keep a lookout for his friend in case he did manage to get round to see to the window.

We got back about four thirty and he hadn't arrived. I scurried around with a duster and then went upstairs to make Ken's bed. I hated touching anything that had come into contact with his body and always put it off. His shirts and dirty underwear were worse. I had to force myself to pick them up from the floor where he flung them. But it wasn't dirty underwear that met my eyes when I entered the room. Someone had turned out every drawer.

I went into a complete panic. Ken would think it was me. I started frantically to straighten everything and return them to the drawers. It took me an hour and then I went into my own room and saw the same thing had happened there. I didn't know what to do. Chrissie's room was the same.

I hurried downstairs straight to the den. There were marks on the door, marks I hadn't made with my careful levering of the knife but harsh indentations which had splintered the wood. The door was still locked however. Whoever it was hadn't managed to force their way in.

I picked up the phone and then replaced it and went to see if Mr. Jennings was still working in the garden. He'd gone inside and the impetus that had sent me running to him faltered before the prospect of knocking on the door and perhaps involving his wife in explanations. I didn't know her as I knew her husband. She was never friendly. If those marks hadn't been made on the door I would have cleared up everything and not said a word but Ken would see them.

I went back to the phone and called the police.

When Ken got back he was furious. The police had stayed for a little while asking questions and then told me to get Ken to phone them if anything was missing.

They hadn't acted at all as I'd expected. There was no attempt to take fingerprints of anything for a start. Just a cursory glance inside the bedrooms and then a look at the door. They made me feel as if I'd made a fuss about nothing and when Ken started on me I was ready to cry.

"I had to phone them," I protested. "Don't you realize? Someone's been in this house. They tried to get into your den. Look at the marks on the door."

"Are you quite sure you didn't do that yourself?" he said silkily.

"I knew you'd think that."

"Why?"

I backed away. "You do think it, don't you?

Well, I didn't. I didn't." I rushed into the kitchen, venting my feeling on the pots and pans.

He wasn't going to get dinner at seven. I heard him phoning the police, saying smoothly that nothing was missing. He hadn't even checked. But a little later I heard him going into the den.

At eight o'clock I put the dinner on the table and called him. He came out and ate it in silence and then told me he wanted me to go into Manchester the next day and choose some perfume.

I stared at him in surprise. "Can't you get it yourself?"

"No doubt," he said coldly. "But I'm not going to make a fool of myself sniffing at dabs of scent. Mrs. Singer will be here to look after Chrissie. You can spend the morning in town."

"Is the perfume for Mrs. Singer?"

"What business is that of yours?"

I shrugged. "I would have thought if it was for her you could find something in the chemist's shop here."

"The lady speaks! It wouldn't be good enough for you, would it? Not with your expensive tastes. It's time you stopped looking down your nose at other people, setting yourself up above them as if you were something special. You're what I've made you. Don't forget that. I've bought those clothes on your back, I've paid for everything that's made you what you are."

I stared at him in resentment. He had. It was true. But not for my sake but his own. I couldn't ever wear jeans and a sweater. I couldn't ever walk down to the shops without being in bandbox condition. My appearance was a reflection on himself. I had to look good. I was part of his shop window.

The sharpness went from his tone. He said smoothly, "But that's by the way. I'm sure you don't need reminding of your obligations. Spend about £5 on it. And get a dress for yourself as well. Summer is coming. You'll want something new."

"I don't need anything," I said sullenly.

"So you'll make a scarecrow of yourself and have people thinking I'm neglecting you now your mother's dead. Get it—and some stockings or whatever it is you young girls wear nowadays. You had a ladder the other day. I don't like slovenliness."

I sighed. It wasn't worth arguing about it.

70

I'd get a dress, and some tights. I didn't like slovenliness myself. It was just the fact that he paid for everything I had that made me want to do without.

I went up to town wondering if I could get some kind of job that he wouldn't find out about. It would be nice to have some money that I could call my own and not have to account for every penny, for although Ken was generous with his housekeeping money I had to note down exactly what I spent. He never gave me money for anything else. He had never given my mother any either. It was all charged, so that he could check the accounts.

I went straight to Kendals and went upstairs first to choose a dress. My heart wasn't in it and I didn't see anything I liked except for a very expensive navy and jade linen. Normally I would have hesitated but not after what Ken had said. Besides I couldn't go anywhere else. Kendals was the only place where I had an account.

I got my tights next. A dozen pairs. That would teach him to complain about ladders.

And then the perfume. I took my time choosing that. Despite Ken's claim of my expensive tastes mine was usually out of the Yardley range.

I finished up with Ma Griffe. It was a waste on Mrs. Singer but Ken would approve. Did I dare get some for myself? I hesitated and then decided it wasn't worth it and went to the food department.

I never left Kendals without feasting my eyes on the exotic things they had in that food store. It was like nowhere else I had ever visited in the North. Strange, weird foods from all over the world, luxury items, peaches in brandy, truffles, caviare, a whole range of frozen meals that promised to delight a gourmet. I drooled over them for a good fifteen minutes and then bought some chocolate biscuits for Chrissie. They weren't particularly exotic but a brand not often seen in Carsdale, and they weren't very expensive.

I'd gone up the steps and was heading for the King Street exit when someone touched me lightly on the shoulder.

It was a man, dark and tanned with very blue eyes. He said softly, "I wouldn't go outside if I were you. Not unless you want to be arrested the moment you step through the door."

72

"I beg your pardon." I stared at him blankly. I couldn't believe I'd heard right.

"There's a store detective on your tail right now. Look in your bag."

"You must be mad." He spoke with an American accent and his clothes were the casual sports shirt, light slacks and coloured golfing jacket that the Americans seem to wear so much in their films. "Are you implying I've stolen something?"

"Let's not have a song and dance about it," he said. "Just look in your bag."

"You look." I thrust my open shopping basket at him.

"I think you have a clear conscience," he said and a small smile lightened his dark face. "Come with me. I'll straighten this out."

He took my arm, and my shopping bag, and led me back down the stairs and through the subway to the perfume counter.

I was too startled to resist at first and then when I got my wits back and started a slightly incoherent speech of protest he said casually, "Let's not have a commotion. Keep your dignity."

At the counter he leaned across to the girl

and said softly, "What were you told about this young lady?"

The girl looked startled. Her gaze went beyond us and the man turned. He beckoned. "I thought so. You're one of the store detectives, aren't you?"

A smartly dressed woman in her mid-forties had come up behind and was regarding him warily. He didn't give her time to answer. He said, "Now I saw a girl slip something into this young lady's shopping bag and then speak to the assistant here when she'd walked away with her purchase. It didn't take much imagination to realize she was being set up for something she didn't do."

"I think perhaps it would be better if we conducted this conversation in the manager's office," the store detective said, not committing herself to anything.

"By all means." The man was very much in command of the situation and he remained so.

Half an hour later we were outside Kendals and he was leading me into a coffee bar across the street. Inside my bag had been two boxes of Worth. I hadn't been able to believe it. I still found it difficult to take in that but for this man I would have been arrested and right now it could have been a police station I was sitting in.

"Who could have done it? Who would do a thing like that?" I must have said it a dozen times. The girl hadn't been able to give much of a description. She'd been too taken aback and then too occupied in keeping tabs on me until the store detective could take over.

The man couldn't give much of a description either. He'd only seen her from the back. She'd been wearing a head scarf and a loose coat.

The manager had thanked him for preventing them from making a mistake but I felt tainted as I walked out of his office. "They could have thought we were acting together," I said. "They work as a team sometimes, don't they? Did you think that too? Is that why you said that about my having a clear conscience?"

"It crossed my mind," he said. "But you didn't look the type. Then when I spoke to you your reactions were all wrong. I thought for a moment I was going to get my face slapped. There I've brought a smile. I wondered what you'd look like with one." He patted my hand. "You're not cut out to be a tragedy queen. Now forget about it."

"Why did you wait? Why didn't you say something right away?"

"I wasn't sure. I thought it better to follow you for a little while."

"To see if I'd try to steal something else?"

"My! You are bitter and twisted. It takes courage for a man to put himself forward, you know. I'm the shy type." His eyebrows went up. "You don't believe me? I was watching you for quite ten minutes wondering how I could make your acquaintance. How do you think I was in such a handy position to see what that girl did to you?"

"You were watching *me*?"

"Why not? You're a very attractive sight to behold. I'm a stranger here. I don't know many people. Now I know you. I tell you, you can curse that girl as much as you like but to me she was a godsend. *Now* you'll have lunch with me, won't you? You can't possibly refuse. But if I'd stepped up to you there in Kendals and asked you, I think I might very possibly have got that slap across the face."

I laughed. "Not a slap. That is far too extreme. Perhaps a frozen glacier-like stare." And perhaps not. I wondered, but not aloud. He was a very attractive man; with an assurance backed up by more than his dark good looks. Possibly he had money, or a job that gave him authority over others. Certainly he was used to command. The episode in the store had proved that. There he had been forbidding, even a little alarming. In a relaxed mood he was different again. His very blue eyes dominated his face, softening the harshness of features that would otherwise have been formidable. They were eyes of experience, eyes that had seen a lot. He was, I thought, about thirty. And he definitely wasn't the shy type.

We exchanged names and he told me he was over from Texas for a holiday. He was staying in the country with some friends and had come into Manchester to see what the big city had to offer.

We had lunch and then he saw me to the station. He didn't say anything about seeing me again which rather cast a shadow on what had turned out to be a lovely day. I liked him. I had never met anyone like him before. Lee Dexter. It was an effort not to look back once I had passed through the barrier and I got into the train telling myself that I'd probably talked too much. I'd practically told him my life history. It must have bored him to tears.

Next time I meet a man like that I told myself miserably, concentrate on him. Be a listener instead of a talker. But he had made it so easy. He had seemed interested.

I stared unseeingly out of the window. What did I have to look forward to in life? It would be years before Chrissie was able to stand on her own feet. Years and gears of living with Ken. I'd be an old maid before I could leave him. And then what would I do?

The stations flashed past. I was so immersed in misery that my stop had gone before I realized it and then I had nearly an hour's wait before I could get a train back again from the next station.

I crossed over the bridge, mad at myself and the whole world. I'd had to buy another ticket. That meant some dodging with the housekeeping money unless I told Ken. I wasn't going to do that. And I wasn't going to tell him what had happened to me in town either.

I paused, feeling a sudden dryness in my throat. The Manchester train had just roared away beneath me. And Lee was walking across the platform.

From my vantage point high on the bridge he was easily recognizable I watched him hand in his ticket and then cross to the car park. He went to a yellow Capri and seconds later it slid smoothly out into the street.

My knees had a cotton-wool feeling as I slowly went down the iron steps. He'd said he'd been watching me. He hadn't said it had been much longer than ten minutes. From the station right into Manchester. No, longer than that. He must have waited for me outside the house to be able to pick me out. And had a girl really put that Worth in my bag? Or had that been engineered by him too? A fine way of getting to know me. But why? And I had prattled on like a fool. Had I told him everything he wanted to know?

I felt sick with chagrin. How could I have been so trusting, falling for his practised charm? I had made it so easy for him.

I walked through the town and up towards the hill. Was that burglary connected somehow? Was he perhaps the brother who had asked so many questions? The vicar had distrusted him. Naturally enough he hadn't been distracted by dark good looks and masculine charm. An American accent could be assumed and it wasn't as if he'd told me a lot about himself. Just that he was from Texas and staying with friends. I could hardly trip him on that. And he wouldn't have expected I'd do such a fool thing as to miss my stop. The service was an hourly one. He'd expect me to be well away from the station by then.

Mrs. Singer was in the garden. She had got one of the deckchairs out and was basking in the sunshine. We were doing very well in the weather this Easter. There was no sign of Chrissie.

I didn't disturb her right away. I went inside the house. She'd made the bed in Ken's room and that seemed to be about all. The lunch dishes were still in the sink but the window had been mended in the dining-room. The new glass was smudged and needed cleaning.

I had a bath and changed into a sweater and slacks. Chrissie was next door again with Libby. I could see her through my bedroom window.

I went out and stood before Mrs. Singer. She appeared to be extremely comfortable. It was almost a shame to disturb her.

"Had a good day, Mrs. Singer?"

She shot up as if I'd roared down her ears. "Oh! Nell! I wasn't expecting you back so soon."

"No? Actually I'm much later than I'd intended. Ken only gave me the morning off."

She laughed as if I'd made an extremely funny joke. It faded nervously as I stared at her and her hands went to her hair, patting and teasing the whispy tendrils into place. I couldn't see what Ken saw in her. She was good barmaid material, big-breasted, brassy, quick with her tongue . . . usually. Just now she seemed to be at a loss for something to say. My stare upset her. I felt a sense of gratification that in some way alleviated my humiliation at the hands of Lee Dexter and I did nothing to relieve the situation.

She had been brought in by Ken to teach me how to cook. All right. She should show me. I was chillingly polite. She found her tongue again and talked, volubly and nervously. I watched her and her hands fumbled and fluttered, all fingers and thumbs. For someone reputed to be such a good cook and house-keeper she was amazingly inept. She stuck it out for about an hour and then Chrissie came bounding in and innocently added to her ordeal with the inevitable questions that only a child can think of. In an exasperated moment she

81

sliced the top of her thumb with the vegetable knife as she was dicing the carrots.

I didn't even feel any remorse then although she had gone white at the sight of her own blood. "Try the cold tap," I suggested casually, as she merely stared down at the seeping redness.

"I can't stand it," she said numbly. "I can't stand it a moment longer. You're playing with me. Like a cat with a mouse. It wasn't my idea. I didn't—I couldn't—"

I was suddenly ashamed of myself. Taking it out on her because of Lee Dexter, because she was Betty's mother, because of Ken . . . She could have thought she was doing me a favour in teaching me to cook. Ken wouldn't have shown himself in his true colours to her.

"I'm sorry," I said after a long moment. "I'll get you a band-aid."

"You know what you can do with your band-aid. I'm going home. I'm—" She snatched up her bag and coat and rushed out of the house.

Chrissie said soberly, "Is she going to be my new mummy?"

I closed my eyes. God forbid. And said aloud, "What makes you ask that?"

"She was looking through your drawers this morning and when I asked her what she was doing she told me I was cheeky, she had a perfect right to do anything she wanted in this house. I don't like her."

"No, well . . ." Maybe I had done the right thing after all. She wouldn't go on thinking she would like to be Mrs. Ken Manning if she thought she had us to cope with. But I wouldn't have thought it would be so easy to demoralize her.

I went on preparing the meal, wondering if Ken had told her to look through my drawers. It sounded very much like it. Or maybe she had just been curious and said the first thing that came into her head.

Ken was home early. He came bouncing into the kitchen, an expression of almost joyful anticipation on his face. It faded rapidly as he saw me. "Where's Mrs. Singer?" he demanded.

"She went home."

"But I asked her to stay to dinner."

"Really?" I reached up for the plates warming over the stove. "She must have decided to decline your invitation."

"You upset her, didn't you? I warned you. I—"

"She only bought three chops," I interrupted mildly. "She can't have intended staying."

"I told her—She— Oh, the stupid fool." His face went red with anger and he slammed out of the kitchen.

I opened the door quietly. He'd gone to the phone. I listened with a sinking heart. He must be keen to get so angry because she'd turned him down. Dinner with the family. It was putting it on a serious footing.

The anger had gone from his voice. He spoke soothingly. "Now Gladys, don't take on so. It's all right. There's nothing to worry about. So it—" He stopped. I thought he'd seen the open door and moved quickly back to the stove. It was just as well I did. He pushed it open wide and stood staring at me suspiciously.

"Dinner in five minutes," I said.

"I don't want any. Did you get that perfume?"

"It's in your room."

He closed the door with another slam and a few seconds later I heard the front door go.

That was nice. Just Chrissie and I. I called her down and we had dinner and then had a very pleasant evening watching television. Ken hadn't returned when I went to bed and I wedged a chair under my door handle. I wasn't going to be disturbed again if he came in feeling belligerent—as he probably would do once he'd spoken to Gladys. Gladys! What a name.

I dreamed about Lee Dexter and woke with an odd restless feeling which made me angry with myself. The tricks the subconscious play. If I ever did see him again I wouldn't be rushing into his arms.

Ken was in an extraordinary good humour at breakfast. It was one of the moods I distrusted most. He told me Mrs. Singer wouldn't be coming again until Saturday but no mention was made of what she might have said about me. "Had a good day in town yesterday?" he asked.

"It was all right."

"You got everything you wanted?"

"I think so. Did she like the perfume?"

"Oh! Yes. She wanted me to apologize for yesterday. You must have thought her behaviour very peculiar."

He made it a question, waiting for a comment. I shrugged. "I suppose it's understandable."

"Why?" He came back at me like a rocket.

"I don't think I need to spell it out."

"Oh." He leaned back in his chair, a complacent smile spreading out across his face. "You mean she fancies me?"

"Does she?" I raised my eyebrows. "There's no accounting for some people's tastes."

"Now listen here, lady. Your mother had no complaints."

"No, she didn't. And you and I know why, don't we?" I went to the door and called Chrissie. If Mrs. Singer wasn't coming in I knew where we were going. Winters Hall was open on Wednesday afternoon as well as Saturday. I wanted to see that portrait again.

Ken said, "Your mother was a very unusual woman. What did she do before she married your father?"

"I don't know."

"She was very young, wasn't she?"

"Yes." I regarded him suspiciously.

"She never talked much about her earlier life." He paused, and then said affably, "But people don't talk about the things they are ashamed of, do they?"

He'd been talking to Betty again. I wasn't going to rise to his baiting. I said flatly, "I imagine it depends on the individual person. I am quite sure my mother was ashamed of nothing in her past."

"Perhaps, perhaps. I had a few words with the vicar last night. He appears to be rather worried about you."

I froze. Mr. Walton wouldn't have said anything. Surely not.

Ken smiled. "Well, I'll be off. I might be late tonight. I don't know yet."

I waited until he'd driven off and then I went to the phone. I had to know. Ken had meant something by those few words. He'd known they would worry me. And if he did know he'd never let it rest. I could even see him making an approach to the Howards. I shuddered at such a prospect.

Mr. Walton was out. I phoned again after Chrissie and I had finished breakfast and this time managed to speak to him.

No, he hadn't told my stepfather about the portrait but Ken had asked him what had happened at Winters Hall. He'd been rather concerned about the attack I'd made on Betty. "I told him that you wouldn't have hurt Betty," Mr. Walton said earnestly. "I must have a word with her as soon as possible. She seems to have made out that she was in danger of being murdered. That type of girl does tend to exaggerate I'm afraid. It's a great pity. Rumours start flying about and cause a great deal of trouble and unhappiness."

"I posted the letter to Somerset House yesterday."

There was a resigned oh, followed by silence. I could almost see him chewing unhappily at his lip.

"That brother of Miss Howard's," I said. "What did he look like?"

"A pretty boy," the vicar said unexpectedly.

"Pretty?" I prompted doubtfully as he seemed to leave it at that.

"Well, perhaps that wasn't the right word to use," he said hesitantly. "He was dark and good looking. Very charming. I imagine few people could refuse him anything. Why do you ask? Has he been to see you?"

"I don't know." Lee Dexter didn't quite fit that description. I couldn't imagine anyone ever calling him a pretty boy. But he was dark and good looking and charming. I couldn't see many people refusing him anything either. "You said boy. Was he young then?"

"I should say about twenty two or twenty three."

That settled that. Mr. Howard was hardly masquerading as an American called Lee Dexter then. Not unless one of us was very bad at estimating ages.

"If he does call," Mr. Walton said and then I didn't hear any more. A yellow Capri had pulled up outside the house and a second later Lee Dexter got out and started to walk up the path.

4

I MUST have said good-bye to Mr. Walton. I would surely not have been so rude as to put the receiver down when he was in the middle of telling me something—but I would never have been able to swear to it. I was utterly and completely transfixed; a myriad of emotions sweeping through my body. Impossible to analyse which was stronger. A nervous excitement perhaps. I watched him every step of the way, scarcely breathing. When the doorbell went it ran through my body like an electric current.

I didn't move. I don't think I could have done if I'd wanted to.

After a moment it rang again. Chrissie was in the kitchen wiping the breakfast dishes and she called out, "Shall I go?"

"No."

"But, Nell . . ." She came out, the tea towel in her hand. "Aren't you going to see who it is?"

"I know who it is." But I didn't. And I

wasn't going to find out by hiding from him. That wasn't being very clever.

The bell rang for a third time and Chrissie said uncertainly, "He p'raps knows we're in. Maybe he can hear the radio."

"All right. Let him in. Give me a minute though." I was up the stairs in a flash, changing into my new dress, hurriedly making up my eyes and mouth, giving my hair another brush. Shoes . . . Where were my navy shoes? I found them at the back of the wardrobe but they needed polishing. The polish was in the kitchen. Blast and dammit. My sandals then. A squirt of Sea Jade, a final glance at my reflection. A handkerchief to rub palms which had suddenly become moist and clammy. And then the slow descent down the stairs.

Chrissie was being the hostess, offering coffee. "It's not really cold," she was saying. "We have only just finished breakfast."

The lazy Texan drawl seemed even lazier. He knew the right words to say to Chrissie. He would probably know the right words to say to anyone.

I stopped on the bottom step to take a deep breath. He wasn't going to know that I had seen him in Carsdale yesterday. I was going to be clever about it. This time I would be the one to find out about him.

He stood up as I entered the room.

Chrissie exclaimed, "Oh, what a lovely dress, Nell. When did you get that?"

"Oh, I've had it ages," I said, giving a quelling glance which was completely lost on her but unfortunately didn't escape Lee.

He smiled, his eyes crinkling at the corners. "Hi there."

"Hello." I was striving for poise but only too well aware of the flush that hadn't been wholly brought about by Chrissie's lack of tact.

"You've—" She was beginning to let something else out of the bag too. I could tell.

I said hurriedly, "I think we'll have fresh coffee, Chrissie. Do you think you can make it?"

"Of course," she said aggrieved at my own tactlessness. "I'm not a baby." She picked up the percolator, reluctant to leave the room, perceptive enough to feel she would be missing something.

"Go on then." I sat down, consciously striving for a graceful pose. "How did you know where to find me?" Let him talk his way out of that.

It was almost as if he knew what I was thinking. "We gave our names and addresses to the manager of that store. Don't you remember?"

So we had. Now what had he given for his? I'd been too flurried to notice what he'd said.

His smile deepened. "You don't imagine I'd have let you go without knowing where I could get in touch with you again?"

I blushed again. If I hadn't seen him at the station I would have lapped that up. As it was, it was still an effort to remind myself that he was playing some kind of game where I had to be the victim. He was too plausible, too . . . too . . . I didn't know. He was too much for me—that I knew.

"It's a little early for a morning call, isn't it?"

"It depends on what you have in mind. I thought perhaps you would like to spend a day in the country with me. Chrissie too," he added as she came into the room. "It's a lovely day for a drive."

"Yes, we have been very lucky with the weather this Easter." I didn't need to ask Chrissie if she wanted to go. Her eyes were shining like stars. "Did you have anywhere special in mind?"

Chrissie answered before he could commit himself. "We were going out for the day anyway today. To Winters Hall. We went there on Saturday but Nell had an accident. She didn't see it properly."

"An accident?" he repeated slowly.

"It was nothing much. I fell down the stairs."

"She was unconscious," Chrissie said dramatically.

"No, no, I'd fainted that was all. I think the coffee will be ready now, Chrissie."

"So you want to go back there?" He sat down, his eyes on my face.

"Not if you have somewhere else in mind." I was sure he didn't. I wondered how he would have worked round to taking us there if Chrissie hadn't come out with it. For he would have done. I knew it as if he'd spoken his intention aloud. He didn't ask where it was. The car nosed its way through the traffic without hesitation and he drove with only perfunctory glances at the signposts.

We had an hour in Lyme Park and took a walk to see the daffodils and then we had lunch at an old posting house. He excused himself at the end of the meal and was away about ten minutes. I went to the ladies room and saw him coming away from the telephone. He was frowning, his jaw set hard, and then he saw me and the easy mask slipped into place again as he smiled. "We've got plenty of time," he said. "Would you like to see the village first? It's only a small place but very picturesque."

"Have you been to the Hall before?"

"Yes."

"Why didn't you say? You can't want to waste your time over here going over the same ground. We'll go somewhere else. There are plenty of places of interest around here."

"No. Winters Hall it is."

"But—"

"Don't argue. It's what you want."

And what he wanted too. I watched him go back to the table. The phone call had displeased him. Who had he called? And why? Was he marking time by going to the village first? If so, for what reason? The Hall opened at two o'clock. It would be open now.

I was feeling sick and nervous. It was a strain trying to act naturally but I didn't argue any more.

We saw the village, a little hamlet of scattered houses and farms, a main street which took about ten minutes to saunter down, two or three shops, a café which promised fresh cream teas, a pub, the church, and then we turned to the Hall.

It was after three and the car park was half full.

"I don't suppose you want to go through the house again, Chrissie," Lee said. "Shall you and I go to the mere and have a boat ride?"

Such an invitation was irresistible and he must have known it. So I was to go alone.

It was what I had wanted and yet because Lee had suggested it I hesitated. His eyes were on me, it was almost an appraisal but there was something else too. Regret? Reluctance? Perhaps not. But an expression akin to those things. I had it suddenly and because I would never have associated it with the man I felt a finger of fear touch the back of my neck. It was apprehension. He must have seen something in my own face that revealed my awareness. For a fleeting moment I thought he was going to say something, give me some kind of warning but he regretted the weakness at once and turned abruptly.

They walked away, Chrissie holding his hand, her flower-like face upturned to his.

I felt deserted. No word of when I would

see them, how long they would be. I was left completely on my own.

Beryl Howard didn't recognize me. She was busy being charming to a party of Germans. I slipped in behind them and stayed in their wake. There was no sign of Madeleine but I heard her voice as we started to mount the first lot of stairs.

I went back to stand in front of the portrait of Jasper Morrison, staring at the shadowed face. There was an elusive familiarity about that now but I couldn't have seen that before. Not if it had only been discovered five years ago.

The Long Gallery was empty of people when I mounted the stairs again. I went through the linen cupboard. I'd not planned what I would do but this had to be the first step. The memory of that man's distress had haunted me.

He was by the window and though he didn't turn he knew it was me. "I hoped you'd come up," he said in a low voice.

I went towards him slowly and stood by his side. Now I knew who Lee had telephoned. He had a pair of binoculars in his hands but the attic windows overlooked the mere, not the front of the house. There were three boats bobbing about on the placid surface. I took the binoculars from him and held them to my eyes. Lee was rowing in one of the boats with Chrissie leaning back blissfully, trailing her hand in the water.

"He phoned you, didn't he? He told you we were on our way." I turned towards him, raising my eyes. It was the hardest thing I'd ever had to do, but it must have been even harder for him. He stood like granite, the clear light of the sun on his ravaged face. "I'm sorry I ran away on Saturday. I meant to come back."

"It doesn't matter." His eyes were deep-pitted and dull and flat, as if he had known a lot of pain. As indeed he must have done. Almost the whole of his face was composed of a ridged scar tissue, his mouth was just a gash with no recognizable lips.

He moved away as if he could bear my gaze no longer and went to sit in the winged chair again.

I walked over to the piano, idly letting my fingers find their own melody. "*Did* you send Lee to find out about me?"

"Do you mind so very much?" he said in a low voice. "I couldn't go out myself."

Of course he couldn't. Not with that face, afraid so much of letting people see him. I said,

"I don't mind telling my life history to anyone. I've got nothing to hide. What I do mind is the way it was done. There was no need for all that —and the break-in too! Did Lee do that?"

"Break-in?" he questioned, his voice rising in surprise.

"Someone went through our house. Nothing was taken—at least I don't think so. They just made a mess, turning out all the drawers and everything."

"Lee wouldn't have done that," the man said with an emphasis that was convincing.

"And the bother at Kendals? He didn't arrange that either?"

"He told me about that," the man said slowly. "It happened just as he described it."

"Someone wanted me put away for a while. I wondered if it could be connected with my visit here. Maybe someone thinking I was going to make a nuisance of myself. Why should Madeleine send her brother to the vicar to find out where I lived under the pretext of asking how I was. That's not normal behaviour. Nothing's been normal since my visit here on Saturday. Why did you want to know more about me? Was it my name? Or because I seemed to know this room?"

"I knew your mother."

My fingers stilled on the keys. "And my father too?"

"Yes."

I stared straight ahead of me. "I never knew him. He was killed before I was born. That is his portrait at the head of the stairs, isn't it?"

"Yes."

"My mother had a photograph of him—just the same. I tried to find it but Ken must have thrown it away. She loved my father very much."

"But she married again." Again. So she had been married. I was no bastard child. I got up and went over to the window, staring at the scene outside without really seeing it. "I think she felt she she had no alternative. I was running wild, I wasn't turning out the way she thought my father would have wanted. Her whole life was governed by the determination to make me a lady because of my father. I think she made a bargain with my stepfather. She couldn't have loved him. No one could love Ken Manning."

"She bore him a child."

"Yes, she did." I glanced down at the lake and could just make out Chrissie's golden head.

"And she was barely forty years of age when she died. It was only a cold—but she didn't take care and it developed into pneumonia. She could have fought it but she didn't. She thought she'd achieved what my father wanted; she died with his name on her lips."

"When was this?"

"At Christmas time." I leaned my forehead against the cool glass. A strange conviction was growing in me—strange, because it was impossible. "Did my mother live here? Here in this room?"

"In your mother's time these attics were a collection of rabbit hutches. All the servants slept here—as they had done for generations."

"She was a servant?"

There was a pause before he replied. "Didn't she ever talk of her life here?"

"She talked about my father—that was all. Never a word about where he came from or what she had done before she was married. Even where she lived before Carsdale. I wasn't curious. It never occurred to me to wonder about it. And then I came to this house, I found this room, I felt I had been here before. And then that portrait. It was an awful shock. I didn't know what to think. I even wondered if my mother had really been married. I wrote to Somerset House to find out because I couldn't find any of her papers at home."

"She was married here in the village church. It was a very simple ceremony. She wore a long white dress she had made herself and she had flowers in her hair. She was very beautiful."

"They didn't have very long together."

"No, they didn't," he agreed quietly.

I was longing to ask who he was—relative, friend or . . . what? But I couldn't bring myself to do it. I couldn't form the words.

"You said she was a servant. What did she do?"

"She came here at thirteen and started as a kitchenmaid but she was bright and quick and very clean and it was decided she'd make a good ladies maid. When Beryl came here as a bride your mother became her personal maid."

"Did she like working here?"

"She never complained. She had a happy nature. She was always singing, always ready to smile, always—" He stopped. "It's a long time ago."

"Yes." I wished I'd known my mother like that. I'd never heard her sing. "Why did she leave here?"

"She had her reasons I suppose."

"Were you here then?"

"No."

"They must have been very strong reasons." I turned away from the window and sat down on one of the deep armchairs. "I suppose the family weren't very kind to her. A kitchenmaid marrying into the family! Did they banish her up here again? Is that why I know this room?"

"I don't know." He leaned forward, pouring himself a drink from a decanter on a table placed conveniently by the side of his chair. His hands shook. I wondered if it was habitual; one of them was badly scarred but it was nothing like the scar tissue on his face.

"Could I have one of those?" I said diffidently.

He was instantly apologetic. "I've been alone so long I've forgotten my manners. I only have brandy I'm afraid."

"That's all right." I didn't care what it was. The alcohol was the important ingredient.

He got up and brought another glass from a small cupboard. "I'll get some water," he said. There was a door, hardly concealed but I'd not noticed it, and he vanished through it.

I heard the running of the tap and then he had closed the door again.

"Is that a bathroom?"

"You—er?" He was disconcerted again.

"Oh no," I said hastily. "I was merely being curious."

He seemed relieved. "There's a bathroom and bedroom—but no kitchen." He gave me the drink and said half to himself. "I thought it had been converted for me. Now I'm beginning to wonder. He tossed his drink back and poured himself another. "Are you happy with your stepfather?"

"No," I said flatly.

"Then why stay with him? You're old enough to make your own life, aren't you?"

"If I leave, he's threatened to send Chrissie into a home."

"Lee said you were at Oxford. Were you planning on teaching?"

"Yes, I think so. I like children."

"Chrissie . . . ? How old is she?" There was pain in his voice. I wondered why.

"Eight years old."

"A nice child?"

"Oh yes! There's nothing of her father in her. She's like my mother in both looks and nature.

I'm not at all like my mother—but you'll see that, I suppose. She used to say I was like my father." I looked down at the brandy, holding the glass between my hands. A rich, smooth liquid that slid down like silk but burned in the stomach. "Were you in a fire?"

"Yes."

"Was it in the war?"

"Yes." He stirred restlessly and jumped like a cat when there was a knock on the door. "Who is it?"

"It's me—Lee. It's getting on for five."

"Oh yes. Come in, Lee."

He came in alone. I said sharply, "Where's Chrissie?"

"In the car. We'd better be going."

I stood up reluctantly. I didn't want to go. "May I come again?"

It was Lee who answered. "I'll bring you."

The man said nothing. I put my glass down and walked to stand in front of him. He seemed to hunch himself down in his chair, keeping his head down and overcome by an impulse that I couldn't explain I stopped and touched his shoulders, pressing my cheek against his ruined skin. "Good-bye," I said unsteadily and I turned and walked past Lee down the stairs.

He'd put the light on. I pushed against the panelling and came face to face with Madeleine. She had a party of about half a dozen people behind her and her jaw dropped in the middle of saying something as she stared at me in astonished silence.

I said weakly, "Hello." It was most inadequate but the only thing that came to mind.

"How—how did you—" She recovered her presence of mind and smiled at the other people. "I don't think you'll be interested in seeing where we keep our clean linen. Will you carry on? I'll catch up with you in a moment."

The group went reluctantly, more than one giving a backward glance, and then Lee came up behind me.

"Hello, Madeleine," he said smoothly.

"You've been up to the flat. You've . . ."

"Yes." He interrupted her, grasping her by the shoulder, a pleasant smile on his lips. "Keep it to yourself, Mad. There are good reasons."

"But—"

He must have increased the pressure. She winced. "All right, all right. I won't say a word."

"Not to anyone, mind you." He transferred

his grip to my arm and I understood why Madeleine had winced. "Come along, Elinor."

"Lee!"

He paused as Madeleine took half a step after us. "I'll expect an explanation tonight."

"Will you?" He grinned at her. "I don't think I'll be back until quite late."

"I'll wait up for you," she said grimly.

"You do that." He steered me down the gallery, glancing back over his shoulder. "Remember! Not a word."

"You may remove your hand," I said tartly. "I have a dislike of being forcibly removed as if I were a criminal. Are you staying here? Are these those friends in the country?"

"Yes, to both questions."

"This wasn't the address you gave in Kendals." Inattentive I may have been but I wouldn't have missed that.

"No, it wasn't," he agreed without a trace of apology or contrition. And he didn't remove his grasp on my arm either. Not until we'd reached the car.

Chrissie was down on the floor, peeping through the window as if playing a game of hide and seek. "Daddy's here," she announced. "I thought I'd better not let him see me."

I didn't bother asking why. I knew Ken. But Lee didn't. "Why did you do that?" he asked curiously.

She looked at him with vague eyes. She couldn't explain. "I don't know."

I looked for Ken's car. It was over in the corner of the car park. She hadn't made a mistake.

"He's a bit late to see over the house," Lee said. "They close at five." He gazed at the car and then turned back to look at the house. "I wonder . . ." He didn't finish what he was going to say, remaining stilled in thought. Then he shrugged. "Let's go."

He'd have done more than wonder if he knew Ken Manning as I did. I got into the car, apprehension hanging over me like a veiled cloud. Had he put two and two together? He wasn't the type to look around stately homes for the pleasure of it.

Lee drove swiftly back to Carsdale with Chrissie providing most of the conversation. She'd enjoyed the afternoon and prattled on happily, fortunately requiring little in the way of answers from me for my brain was buzzing away with questions which her presence prevented me from asking. I forgot Ken. I wasn't interested in him.

"Can you come round tomorrow morning?" I asked Lee as he pulled up outside the house.

"I was going to ask you to have dinner with me tonight," he said.

"I can't. There's Chrissie."

"But won't your stepfather be home?"

"It doesn't make any difference. I can't go out at night. He doesn't like it."

"I see." He regarded me in silence for a few seconds and then said, "Very well. I'll see you tomorrow. About ten."

We got out of the car. Chrissie waved as he drove off but I didn't move, not until the yellow car turned the corner and disappeared from sight. What was he to the Howard family? More than just a friend? Madeleine was waiting up for him. Well, she wouldn't have to wait very long now. What would he tell her? Why the secrecy? Why . . . What . . . How . . . ?

I was dizzy with the questions and could hardly wait until the following morning.

He arrived a few minutes after ten. I'd made sure Chrissie was out of the way, pushing her to play in the garden with Libby and fortunately she didn't hear the car so we were undisturbed.

I made coffee and Lee sat back in his chair, a thin cigar between his fingers and his long legs stretched out in front of him.

"Did you give Madeleine her explanation?" I asked.

He smiled faintly. "I suppose you feel you have even more right to demand one. All right. You caused quite a stir on Saturday. I didn't know the whole of it. I only heard Madeleine's side of it last night. Although you had mentioned your little accident, I didn't know anyone else had an inkling who you were. I didn't even know if you yourself knew."

"It's about the one thing I had the sense to keep to myself," I said grimly. "How do you think I felt when I realized you'd only got to know me to find out my life history? I saw you, you know, at the station, getting off the next train and going to your car."

"So that's why—" He shook his head, amusement crinkling up the corners of his eyes. "I thought I detected a reserve in your exuberance. Why did you come with me then?"

"To find out what you were up to of course."

I poured out the coffee. "Do you know this house was ransacked too?"

"I didn't. I was told of it last night. You thought I had something to do with it I hear. Do you still think that?"

"I suppose not," I said with some reluctance.

"That's rather a grudging admission."

"Is that so surprising? Does Madeleine have a brother? One who might be described as a pretty boy?"

"You've met him?"

"The vicar has. He told me he received a visit from someone who said he was Madeleine's brother. She was supposed to be concerned about my accident and wanted to know if I was all right. The vicar gave him my address and then began to wonder if he'd done the right thing. He told me to be careful—most unlike the vicar who never thinks bad of anyone—but he thought him too charming." I paused and eyed Lee carefully, "I wondered if that could be you."

"So you think I'm charming?" he asked in amusement. "*And* a pretty boy? Dear me! I'll have to do something about that. That's not the sort of image I care to promote." He lifted the cigar to his lips and blew out a thin stream of smoke. "The visit was genuine enough. Madeleine was curious but she was also concerned about the effects of the fall you had. She has a very tender heart. She's your cousin, of course."

I swallowed convulsively. "I did wonder."

"Her brother—the pretty boy—is Patrick. He is next in line for the Howard estate. You can see why he was so interested in what Madeleine had to say about you. And why he didn't mind going out of his way to find out something about you."

"I don't understand," I said in bewilderment.

"Don't you, Elinor?"

He leaned his head back against the chair, regarding me through half closed eyes. "Do you know what I expected your first question to be?"

I knew what he meant. The question that had been burning in my brain more than any other. Who was that man with the maimed face and hand, who had known my mother and described her with such pain in his voice?

"You think I've guessed, don't you? But what I'm thinking is impossible. And he said he knew my father."

"And who else has any more right to make

such a claim? Your instincts were sound enough. I thought he'd told you when you said good-bye like that."

"He didn't tell me. He didn't even hint at it."

I felt numbed with shock but I'd known, of course I'd known. The conviction had grown stronger and stronger as we'd talked.

That man was my father.

5

"BUT he's dead. My father is dead," I said aloud.

Lee said soberly. "The war was over before anyone knew any different. He'd been hidden by a French family; they'd looked after him and cared for him as best as they could but he'd nearly been burned to death when his aircraft caught fire. Escape was out of the question for such a marked man, even if he'd been able to attempt it. He was very ill for a long time and nearly out of his mind with the pain. They couldn't do much to relieve it. A doctor might have brought the Gestapo down on them. So he stayed hidden in a room little bigger than a cupboard until France was liberated."

He was silent for a little while, giving me time to absorb this, and then he said, "He's not told me all this. He can't talk about that time. Most of what I've learned has come from Madeleine. She told me how long he was in hospital and how much he suffered and then when he came home he found his wife had left

114

him, gone off with another man. She couldn't even bring herself to see him. She left a message saying she was sorry but she couldn't bear the thought of it."

"But that's not true," I cried.

"He doesn't blame her. He doesn't blame anyone for not being able to look at him. He'd gone too long without proper medical attention. That's why they couldn't do anything for him. Plastic surgery wasn't what it is now."

"My mother would never have been so callous; never in a thousand years. And she didn't have another man—only me."

"You were a little young at the time."

"So I couldn't know—that's what you're saying, isn't it? But I knew my mother."

"Well, I'm not here to discuss the moral values of your mother. We'll let that pass."

"What are you here for then? Who are you to my father?"

"I'm here . . . let's say, as a friend to both of you. He would like you to return to Oxford if that's what you want to do. He feels that some arrangement can be made with your step-father whereby Chrissie won't be made to suffer."

"Some arrangement? Financial arrangement

you mean?" I smiled bitterly. "Ken is not short of money. That's not the reason he keeps me at home. Was he going to see my . . . my father yesterday?"

"No. He didn't speak to anyone—not to my knowledge anyway. I couldn't ask outright. You understand, your father didn't want me to talk about you. Not until he was quite sure you were his daughter. Even then I don't think he meant to say anything. He couldn't bring himself to tell you. He was afraid you would be horrified and never want to see him again."

I was silent, remembering how I had run from him.

"He didn't know about the existence of a daughter," Lee went on gently. "No one told him. When you walked in that room he thought he was dreaming. He sees no one but the family and not very much of them. Then when you told him your name it was a terrible shock to him. Your mother's favourite name was Elinor. She always said their first girl would have that name." He paused and then added slowly, "The first boy was going to be Nicolas. They planned on four altogether. Your father talked more that night than I would have believed possible. I realized how much of his life had been smashed. Jasper's curse has a lot to answer for."

"You believe in that? I—" The implication hit me like a thunderbolt. "Are you saying my father is the owner of Winters Hall?"

"I thought I'd made that clear."

"You mean when you said that about Patrick? You mean that I— Oh no!"

"It's quite an inheritance." Lee watched me narrowly but I could only stare at him. "It will be yours one day," he went on. "It's not entailed in the male line."

"How could he not know he had a daughter? How could that be kept from him?"

"He was a broken man remember. I imagine it was easy enough. His mother was alive then. It would have been her doing. She can't have approved of the marriage. In fact, I know she didn't. I've heard enough about her to know she was one of those dyed in the wool snobs to whom the name and the line were all important. She would never have been able to forget her daughter-in-law started out as a kitchenmaid. I feel rather sorry for Beryl right now for of course she must have known. Anyway," he rose to his feet, "I've given you enough to think about. You'd better discuss this with your stepfather and then I think a meeting should be arranged. Saturday perhaps. I'll give you a ring on Friday night."

"Ken isn't going to like this."

"We'll see."

"You might." I faced him calmly enough although his assumption that I didn't know what I was talking about stung once more. Did he think I was a child with no understanding of human nature? I knew my mother. I knew she would never have left my father no matter how badly he'd been scarred. And I knew Ken too. I was dependent on him and he liked it that way. He wouldn't take kindly to any difference in the status quo.

"I don't want him to meet my father," I said slowly.

"Why?"

"He likes to hurt people; he likes to be the one with the upper hand, manipulating, pulling the strings. He'll tell lies about my mother if it serves his purpose. He has an instinct for knowing what will wound the most deeply. My father has been hurt already, in both mind and body. I believe . . . I feel that finding me has brought him some happiness. There was a bond between us from the start. I felt it and I'm sure he did too. We can meet without Ken knowing —without anyone knowing. I don't want to be the heiress of Winters Hall. I don't want my father to acknowledge me. I feel it can only bring trouble."

"You can't hide it," Lee said with a hint of impatience in his voice. "You're his daughter. How can you meet without anyone finding out? Madeleine knows now, and Patrick could have found out. There's Beryl too. She might have thought you lost in obscurity but your father won't let her remain in blissful ignorance for long. He's a very angry man at this moment. He won't forgive her for hiding your existence and he won't let her think she's got away with it either."

"What's done is done. Nothing he can say can bring back the empty years. You must tell him that. Recriminations are pointless."

"Do you want to remain here? Dominated by a man you profess to dislike intensely."

"Dislike!" I gave a short laugh. "That's the understatement of the year. I hate him, I despise him. But he has me in the hollow of his hand. I love Chrissie. Can't you understand? I'll do anything to prevent her life being spoiled."

"She's his daughter. How could he spoil her life?"

"You don't understand. You don't understand at all. Please . . . I know what's best. Don't bring him into this."

"It's impossible to keep him out." Lee touched my shoulder regarding me gravely. "You have your own life to consider Your father can give you security, your independence, any thing you want."

"And what can he give Chrissie? You think I can abandon her? Go back to Oxford without a thought for what Ken would do? She's a little girl—she wouldn't understand anything but the fact that I'd left her to be put into a home. What kind of effect would that have on her? It will scar her for the rest of her life."

"I still think we can sort something out." He thought I was dramatizing. The indulgent patronage was showing again. I didn't know what I was talking about. I was being a hysterical teenager. All teenagers rebelled against authority and Ken stood in for his share as the parental figure.

"You think I'm being stupid, don't you? But please do as I ask. It's not your place to make decisions. It's between my father and I. I'd sooner this be kept quiet and I want you to tell him that. I'll see him whenever I can but for Chrissie's sake I'd prefer things to remain just as they are."

"It may be too late."

"Then it's too late." I shrugged. "Will you drop me in the town? I have some shopping to do."

"All right."

I got my coat and called to Chrissie that I was going to the shops. Mr. Jennings was in the garden again and said she'd be all right for half an hour.

Lee drove down the hill without speaking. I wondered if I'd offended him by telling him it wasn't his place to make the decisions but then he'd offended me by treating me like a baby so I didn't try to smooth things over.

He stopped outside the butchers and I gave him a curt good-bye and went in to get the meat for the day. He moved off and then stopped again and when I went out beckoned me over.

"I've seen those legs before," he said.

I followed his gaze. Betty was arranging something in the window opposite. The mini skirt hadn't yet hit Carsdale in any great proportions although it was doing great guns in the bigger towns but Betty's skirt was so tight it had ridden well up her thighs. I didn't think it a sight worth stopping for but then I was prejudiced. I said shortly, "The pleasure is all yours."

"You know her?"

"Yes."

"And there's no love lost between you?"

"You could say that. She—" I stared at him, the penny dropping at last. "She's the girl in Kendals?"

"I very much think so."

I didn't pause for thought. I was steaming across the road like a bull after a red flag.

Either Betty felt the hot blast of my anger or some instinct for danger made her glance round. She froze for an instant and then panicked. The tiny dinky cars she was arranging in an intricate pyramid went toppling over her feet and she crushed some of them beyond repair in her haste to get out of the window.

When I burst into the shop she had the counter between us and was cowering behind the slight figure of Mr. Coward, the owner of the shop. His mouth was open and he was staring at her in flabbergasted astonishment. At my entry his eyes swivelled round and his mouth dropped even further.

Betty whimpered. "Don't let her touch me. Don't let her near me."

"Don't worry, Betty," I said between my teeth. "I'm not going to give you what you deserve. I just want to know if you've any explanation before I bring the police here."

"I don't know what you're talking about. Mr. Coward, stop her. She tried to kill me. She's mad."

"I'm mad all right. That was a dirty, rotten trick to play. I could have ended up in prison."

"And that's where you should be," Betty cried shrilly. "People like you should be locked up and put away. Get out of here and leave me alone. I'm the one who should go to the police. I'll tell them what you did to me. I've got witnesses. I can prove it. You think you can hush it up, getting the vicar to preach on to me about spreading malicious gossip, but you're dangerous. I'm not going to be forced to keep silent. I'll tell the world what you did. You'll be sorry."

I took a step forward, my hands clenched at my side, and she uttered a thin scream and ducked behind Mr. Coward, holding on to him for dear life.

The anger in me reached boiling proportions. The top of my head felt as if it were going to be blown off with the pressure. She was making me the aggressor, putting me in the wrong, and Mr. Coward was taking it all in. "Stop it. You—"

And then Lee's hand was on my shoulder, his grip like ice water thrown on to the steam, stemming the furious gush in full spate, his lazy Texan drawl dropping into the sudden electrified silence like cool clear drops of crystal. "I don't think there can be any doubt, but the shop assistant at Kendals will clinch matters. Are you the proprietor of this shop?" His eyes flicked to Mr. Coward who started and said nervously, "Yes, yes."

"And this . . . this girl works for you?"

"Her name is Betty Singer," I muttered.

"Yes, she works for me," Mr. Coward admitted with an apprehensive glance at Betty who had gone chalk white.

"But she wasn't here on Tuesday morning? Right?"

"Why, I—"

"Don't answer them. Don't tell them

anything. They're trying to blame me for something I didn't do." Betty grabbed his arm, pulling on it with the frantic clawing of an animal.

"Betty! For heaven's sake pull yourself together." He tried to free himself, embarrassed and bewildered. "I don't know what's going on but stop it. This is neither the time nor the place for a scene like this."

"I don't think we need take up any more of your time," Lee said pleasantly. "We'll get along to the police station."

"Who are you?" Betty whispered. "I don't know you. I've never seen you before."

"I saw you put that perfume in Miss Howard's bag." Lee smiled at her. "A purely disinterested party with no axe to grind. Didn't you wonder what had gone wrong?"

"You don't know what you're doing. She's no good. She deserves to be put away."

"I think not."

He touched my arm and I turned obediently and walked stiff-legged out of the shop.

"You'll regret it," Betty screamed. "You'd better stop him, Miss Nose in the Air. I'll tell them everything."

I didn't answer and we had only gone a few

yards out of the shop when she came flying after us. "I mean it. I'll tell them everything."

"You can tell them what you like," I said coldly. I was in control of myself now. She was scared stiff. It was very gratifying.

"But I know more than you think."

"You could know the Encyclopaedia backwards for all I care. Get out of the way."

She took a step backwards, her eyes like blazing coals in her spotted face. "I hate you, Nell Howard. I hate you more than anyone else in this world. And don't think I'm the only one. It wasn't my idea to set you up but I was only too glad to jump at the chance of putting you where you belong. You think you're—" She put her hands over her mouth, the anger fleeing from her face as I interrupted harshly. "What do you mean, it wasn't your idea? Whose was it?" My brain got into gear, working overtime. "Your mother's. Yes, your mother's. That was why she behaved so oddly. She didn't expect to see me back, did she? Three chops! I should have guessed. She wanted me out of the way, didn't she? She wants to marry Ken. She thought I'd stop it. She thought I stood in her way."

"No, no. It wasn't like that." Fright had

replaced the anger. "Mum didn't want me to do it. She was frightened. She—"

"It was Ken then." No guessing now. I knew.

I didn't think she could have gone any whiter but so much colour drained away that virgin snow would have looked dirty against her face. "I didn't say that. Don't you ever say I did. He —He—" She gasped and then set off at a run, past the shop, down the street, heedless of anyone careless enough not to step out of her way, a blind flight, prompted by fear.

I heard my voice from a distance. "I don't think we'll go to the police."

"Your *stepfather* put her up to it?" Lee sounded incredulous.

"I think so."

"I can't believe it."

"Of course not. You've not believed anything I've said about him." I turned away from him. "I've got the rest of the shopping to do."

"But why should he do a thing like that?"

"I don't know." But I had an idea. I'd been in his holy of holies. He was teaching me it didn't pay to meddle.

"What are you going to do?"

"Just leave me alone, will you? It's no business of yours."

I dived into the greengrocers but he was waiting for me when I came out and relieved me of the heavy weight of the shopping bag. "What time does he get home?"

"It's no use thinking you can talk to him. He won't admit a thing with anyone else present. And Betty won't say a word against him. You could see that. She was paralysed with fear at the thought that he might find out she'd said something to point a finger at him."

"What about her mother?"

"Go and see her if you think it will achieve anything. Personally I think it will be a sheer waste of time. She's got less nerve than her daughter."

"I still think we should go to the police."

"No." I spoke with finality. "I can't do that to her, not now. I feel sorry for her. She wouldn't have done it off her own bat. Ken's the one who should pay—but he'll get away with it. You can be sure of that. He has only to deny it if she did manage to screw up the courage to tell the truth. His word against hers. And he's a past master at creating a false image and making people believe him."

"You really do hate him, don't you?" he said slowly.

"I hate him for what he is, and I hate him because I'm so helpless against him."

"I'm sure your father could do something to help you."

"No."

He stared at me. "I feel inadequate for the first time in my life. I don't know what to do."

"There's nothing you can do. Ring me tomorrow. During the day when he's not at home."

"I'll drive you back."

"All right. I've only the bread to get now."

At the house he was still reluctant to leave me but I got out of the car and shut the door decisively. I didn't look back once. I was shutting the door on more than Lee, I was shutting it against my father too. I prayed he would understand but I felt very unhappy as I prepared lunch for Chrissie and myself. No one could understand Ken, no one could believe what he was capable of.

The more I thought about it, the more certain I became that his reason for arranging that charade had been because of the visit I had paid to his den. And maybe it wasn't merely malicious retribution. Maybe he was afraid of what I'd seen.

I called Chrissie in and tried to put Ken out of my mind but it was difficult. Supposing I had been caught as he intended? I might not have been sent to prison, not for a first offence. It would have meant probation though, and a record on file with the police. A blot on my character that would count against me in the future. Was that what he wanted? So that if I ever told anyone what I'd seen in that room the likelihood against being believed was lessened. All that money . . .

Blackmailers make a lot of money.

The thought flashed unbidden into my mind and once there it refused to budge. I could picture Ken as a blackmailer. It was just his metier.

"You're not listening to me," Chrissie said accusingly.

"Oh, I'm sorry. What was that?" I smiled at her but after a few minutes my thoughts were wandering once more and she got up from the table. "I'm not going to talk to you any more."

"But you've not finished your lunch."

"I don't care. I'm going to play with Libby again."

Hurt aggrievement in every step she marched to the door, stopping as the bell rang at the front. Curiosity then vied with her determination to fully register her disgust with me.

I watched her, half smiling, and the bell rang again.

"Shall I answer it?" she asked.

"If you like." I didn't think it would be Lee again. But neither did I think it would be Mrs. Singer.

She brushed past Chrissie as if she didn't exist. Her coat was unbuttoned and she had no make-up on. She was breathing hard as if she'd been running.

I half rose and then subsided again.

She stood at the doorway. "Have you been to the police?"

"No."

"But you're going. You told Betty you were going. You and that man. Who was he? Why should he interfere?"

"Some people don't close their eyes to injustice." I picked up the teapot. "A cup of tea, Mrs. Singer?"

"My God! You're a cool one. I said you knew. I said you knew all along. You were stringing me along, playing with me like a cat with a mouse."

"I didn't know—not until this morning. Chrissie—I thought you were going to play with Libby." She had edged in at the door, half circling Mrs. Singer to stare at her with unconcealed hostility.

"I'm just going." But she didn't move.

Mrs. Singer returned her gaze with dislike. "Little brat," she muttered. "Get going then. I've come to see your sister, not you."

"Maybe you'd better finish your lunch." I wasn't going to have Mrs. Singer ordering Chrissie around in my presence, however much I thought it advisable she removed herself.

Chrissie hesitated and then came back to the table and picked up her knife and fork. She ate stolidly without taking her eyes off Mrs. Singer who fidgeted under her gaze, taking a few steps round the living-room, wheeling around, and teetering back and forth again.

"Are you sure you wouldn't like some tea?" I helped myself to cheese.

"I want to talk to you," she burst out.

"Go ahead."

"Alone."

"Well, do sit down. Chrissie won't be long."

"Can't we go somewhere else? Please."

The *please* was an immense effort on her part. I took pity on her. She did look dreadful. "Come along to the kitchen then."

Once there with the door shut behind her, however, she didn't seem to know where to start.

I leaned against the sink and waited.

Her eyes darted to my face and slid away again. Her hands fluttered nervously, fiddling with her buttons. When at last she burst into speech they were clamped together in an unspoken plea. "Betty's a good girl really. She won't do anything like that again. She won't go around telling anyone you tried to kill her either."

"That is if I don't go to the police?"

"Well, what will you gain by going to them?" She spoke rapidly the words tumbling after one another. "Pigs! The lot of them. They won't thank you for this and it never does anyone any good to get mixed up with them. Ken won't thank you for it. He'll be very annoyed with you."

"I imagine he will—if Betty gets up the nerve to tell the police he put her up to it."

"He—No! What did she tell you? It's a lie.

He never—Oh!" She stared at me, her mouth slack, her eyes fixed blankly.

"It was his idea, wasn't it?"

Her mouth opened and closed like a goldfish, no sound emerging and the sound of the telephone made her jump so violently I thought she was going to take off.

"Who's that? Who's phoning you? If it's your stepfather, don't tell him I'm here."

I went to answer it. It was hardly likely to be Ken but I wasn't going to tell her that.

It was Betty, asking if her mother was there.

I covered the mouthpiece. "Are you here to your daughter?"

She snatched the receiver from my hand. "What have you been saying? You never told—" She stiffened, suddenly intent, her eyes sliding to my face. "All right," she said slowly. "I'll ask her. Yes . . . Yes." She put the phone down after listening for a few minutes and said baldly, "She wants to see you right away."

"She knows where I live," I countered flatly. And she could have asked me herself. No begging for Betty. She couldn't bring herself to do that. She hadn't even tried to sound polite when she'd asked for her mother.

My expression must have told all too clearly

what I was thinking and Mrs. Singer wasn't too proud to beg. I felt sorry for her when I could no longer feel sorry for Betty. "She can't help sounding rude," she said with a catch in her voice, "but she's sorry, really she is. She wants to explain but she doesn't have much time. She'll have to rush back to the shop or she'll get the sack. Mr. Coward won't stand for being left alone when the shop gets busy. Please go and see her. I'll look after Chrissie."

I'd go. But not for feelings of pity. Betty would talk if pressed hard enough. Somehow I knew that.

I got my coat. Chrissie wanted to come with me especially when she learned that Mrs. Singer was staying to look after her.

"I don't need looking after," she said, her lower lip thrusting forward mutinously.

"No, darling, I know. You're a big girl now. But I won't be long. An hour at the most."

"I don't want to stay here, not with *her*." The glance she threw at Mrs. Singer was as hostile as only a child could make it.

I said hurriedly, "Well, go and play with Libby. That's what you intended to do, wasn't it?"

"You left me this morning. You're always

135

leaving me." There was a quiver in her voice that couldn't be ignored and I put my arms around her and pulled her close.

"But I never leave you for long, do I? I always come back—and I always will." I cupped her face in my hands. "Be a good girl."

"All right," she said, albeit with reluctance.

I smiled at her. "That's my darling."

"Are you going to see Lee again?"

"No, not this time. Only Betty. She's asked me to go to her house."

"Oh, Betty!" She pulled a face and I smiled a little, realizing what had been on her mind. She didn't mind being left for Betty. Lee was a different matter. "You liked Lee?"

"I'm going to marry him when I'm grown up. I told him so yesterday." She was very matter of fact about it, and very determined. I kept my face straight.

"And what did he say?"

"He said it was an honour worth waiting for. What did he mean, Nell?"

I laughed, pinching her chin. "It means you're a little minx. I'll see you later."

It started to rain as I walked down the hill, the fine, needle-like drizzle that was so deceptive. By the time I reached the town I was feeling very wet and gratefully accepted the cover of the huge umbrella Mr. Walton proferred as he came out of the vicarage. "I'm going to the post office," he said. "Where are you off to?"

"Betty Singer's."

"Ah yes. Betty." He fell into step beside me. "I suppose it's too early yet for a reply to your letter."

"It doesn't matter now." I hesitated and then said slowly, "I've found my father, Mr. Walton. He's still alive. He didn't know of my existence. He was told my mother had left him for another man and he believed it. He's the owner of Winters Hall."

Mr. Walton was silent for a long time. I didn't interrupt his thoughts and we plodded through the rain down to the shops. "Wait for me," he said outside the post office. "I'll come along with you to Betty's."

"But she—"

I was too late. He'd handed over his umbrella and gone inside.

"I don't think Betty will talk to me with you present," I said when he came out again. "And I want her to talk."

"I see." He eyed me keenly and then said,

"I'll wait for you outside and we can walk back together. There's no point in getting any wetter." He fell into step again, relieving me of the umbrella. "What are you going to do? In regard to your father I mean."

"Nothing. It won't make any difference. I'll try and see him of course—as often as I can— but I'd prefer K—no one to know about it."

"You've not had time to consider it thoroughly yet. You may change your mind. Indeed, I think you will. Elinor, I'd like to talk to you seriously. Come back to the vicarage with me and we'll have some tea."

"Mrs. Singer is looking after Chrissie. I said I wouldn't be long."

"Finish your business with Betty quickly then." He glanced down at me. "What do you want with her?"

I avoided his eyes. "She issued the invitation."

He said with some diffidence, "I talked to her, you know. She's . . . she's difficult to understand."

That meant of course that he was unwilling to believe in pure malice when he met up with it but felt he had to give me some kind of warning.

I stopped outside the house on the corner. It was one of a row of terraced boxes. Further along was the house in which we had lived. Drab, damp houses, two up, two down, lavatory in the backyard, no bathroom, no hot water. And I thought of Winters Hall. Beautiful, serene and gracious. All the comforts of living. And right then I hated the person who had been the cause of my mother's departure. But she was dead—my snobbish grandmother who couldn't bear to have a kitchenmaid daughter-in-law in the same house as herself. How much had she given my mother as a pay off? Enough to buy the house? One or two hundred as conscience money! These houses were at the bottom of the market. They must have been even at the end of the war when the housing shortage was at its most critical.

I knocked on the door and it went away from the pressure of my hand. Betty had left it open for me.

The front room was empty. There was no hall. I went straight through into the room which served as both kitchen and living-room. Betty was in an armchair facing the television which was on at full blast.

"Well?" I said, "I'm here."

139

She didn't appear to hear me. I marched to the television and switched it off, turning to face her.

"Well?" I said again but the belligerence was missing this time and I trailed off uncertainly. Her eyes were wide and unblinking and she didn't move a muscle. Even though the light in the room was drastically reduced by the switching off of the television it didn't look natural.

"Betty?" My voice sank down into a whisper. I knew she was dead, even before I saw the knife buried up to the hilt below her breast.

"Mr. Walton! Mr. Walton!" There was no whisper this time. I was shrieking. My hand went to the knife handle, paused and shrank away. I couldn't touch it, I couldn't touch her. I backed away.

Mr. Walton came in at a run, apprehension all over his face. But whatever he'd been afraid had happened, it wasn't this. He stood disconcerted, as helpless and frightened as I was. "I'll get the police," he whispered finally. "Don't touch anything."

I had no intention of touching anything but when he took off at a run I saw something clasped in Betty's hand that seemed very familiar.

I forced myself to touch that dead hand and prise the fingers open. A handkerchief, that was all it was. But my name was embroidered in the corner. I'd had half a dozen as a Christmas present a couple of years ago.

I stood staring at it, not believing in the evidence of my own eyes and a loud voice said, "All right, miss. We'll take that."

My arms were caught, I was hustled to one side of the room, the handkerchief snatched from my fingers.

Two policemen, the other bent over the body. Lord in heaven! Betty was a body now, not a person. I tried to shake off the restraining hands. "Let go of me. What do you think you're doing?"

"Quiet, you." The one holding me shook me roughly. "Dead, is she?"

"As a nail," the other said laconically.

"You'd better call in." He pulled me round. "What's your name? Why did you do it?"

"Me! I didn't do it." The sick feeling in my stomach was being banished by anger. "Will you let go of me!"

"Elinor," he said, looking at the embroidered name. "That's you isn't it? Elinor Howard."

"Yes, but . . ."

"There's no use denying it. We heard all about it—the quarrelling, the screaming. Quite a fight you had." He glanced round the room. Incredible though it seemed I hadn't noticed the signs of a free for all.

A chair lay on its side, a table lamp was smashed, the debris of pottery lay on the floor; vases, ashtrays, a bowl—anything easily thrown through the air. And yet Betty had been sitting watching television . . .

"You stupid moron," I cried. "Do I look as if I've been in a fight? She was sitting there— just as she is now—when I came in."

His grip tightened on my arms. "So I'm a stupid moron, am I? And you're an innocent little spectator—just passing by. You know nothing about it. You don't even know who she is." He was young, there was down on his cheeks. I doubted if he had to shave every day and yet his eyes were cold and flat and he had a mouth like that of an old embittered man, thin and hard, pulled down at the corners.

"I shall report you," I said in a low furious

voice. "You're exceeding your authority. You're . . ."

"Shut up," he said and pushed me hard into a chair.

I sprawled in an undignified, ungainly heap.

His mouth twitched. He enjoyed the spectacle I made. Slowly, almost lethargically he got out his notebook. "I'll have your statement," he said.

"You'll have the flat of my hand." I bounced out of the chair, exploding with humiliation and anger and brought my hand right across his face. His notebook went flying and his face darkened. "You little bitch. I'll teach you—"

I was shrinking back, out of reach of his predatory hands, when Mr. Walton's voice thundered into the room. It was his best pulpit roar. Bigger men than this beefy policeman had trembled under its impact. "What is the meaning of this?"

The policeman froze and then very slowly turned round, his jaw thrust forward aggressively. A red patch was starting to colour his cheek where I had struck him.

"The do-good vicar!" he said unpleasantly. "Interfering as usual. Well, you can keep out

143

of this one. She was caught red-handed. It's murder."

"Miss Howard and I discovered the body together," Mr. Walton said deliberately. "I left her here while I went to phone the police. It appears your zeal has once again outweighed your common sense, Hadley. I would have thought your last warning might have made you a little more cautious."

So they had met before. And not in very friendly circumstances from the sound of it. Hadley's brow was lowered. He said aggressively, "Cautious! She struck me. That's a serious charge in itself."

"I suppose I'm expected to take your manhandling meekly—just because you wear a uniform." I went to stand by the vicar's side and he put his arm round me. "I shouldn't have left you. Forgive me. I'm afraid the shock addled my wits. Are you all right?"

"She's just committed a murder," Hadley said loudly. "But of course she's all right. Cool as you please."

I felt anything but cool. My knees were knocking together. My wretched temper had let me down again.

"And look at this!" Hadley went on

144

triumphantly. "She was pulling it out of the dead girl's hand." He wafted the handkerchief under the vicar's nose and pointed out the embroidered name. "Elinor! That's her name, isn't it."

"Yes, it is mine," I said, meeting Mr. Walton's questioning eyes with an effort. "But I don't know how Betty got hold of it."

Hadley opened his mouth again but before he could speak the second uniformed man came back into the room. "The inspector's on his way," he said. "Mr. Walton—will you and the young lady wait in the other room please. We have to hang on here," he said to Hadley.

"Yes. Come along, Elinor." Mr. Walton led me into the front room and sat beside me on the flashy mock leather couch.

There were two matching armchairs and together they made the room overcrowded but nevertheless Mrs. Singer had managed to squeeze in two glass fronted display units filled with china and glass animals. There was also a polished wooden coffee table and a stereo unit was against one wall.

When the inspector arrived he had to edge

carefully through the various obstacles before he could sit down to face us.

He folded himself into the chair, a tall man with a thin clever face and tired eyes. His collar was crumpled, his tie knotted carelessly. I stared at his hands. There was a long scar across the back of one of them, red and vivid, scarcely healed.

As if conscious of my stare he turned it over. "My name is Egan," he said. His voice was tired too, quiet, dragging a little. "Detective Inspector Egan." He nodded behind us. "And this is Sergeant Turpin."

I glanced over my shoulder. Another tall thin man, with sharp features and a notebook in his hand.

"I understand you found the body."

I turned back to Egan.

"We found her together," Mr. Walton said firmly.

He was afraid for me, I realized with a shock. Did he think they could believe I had killed Betty in the space of those few minutes when I had been alone in the house with her?

I looked at him and he put his hand over mine, the pressure meant to be reassuring and comforting. But his eyes avoided mine and I felt suddenly cold. He not only thought the police might believe it. He half believed it himself.

6

I TRANSFERRED my gaze to Egan. "Betty phoned me," I said. "She asked me to come and see her. On the way I met Mr. Walton and he accompanied me, to give me the shelter of his umbrella. We had something to discuss so he waited for me outside the house. The door was open. I came in. The television was on at full blast. Betty was in the chair facing it. I thought she was watching and I turned it off and then I saw she was dead. I called for Mr. Walton right away."

I wasn't going to have him telling any lies on my account. My conscience was clear. The police could make what they could out of that. They couldn't find me guilty. It wasn't possible. But there was a niggling fear. That attack at the Hall, exaggerated and distorted by Betty. Lord knew how many people she had told. And my handkerchief clutched in her hand . . . What else would the police find?

There was a constant stream of people going to and from the street to the back room. I heard the pop of flash bulbs, the subdued murmur of voices.

Egan was asking Mr. Walton something. I didn't catch what he said. I'd turned my head and seen the draped stretcher.

I stared down at my hands and suddenly thought of Betty's mother. "Mrs. Singer," I said abruptly. "She's up at our house looking after Chrissie. She'll have to be told."

"She's at your house?" Egan broke off what he was saying and looked at me in surprise.

"Yes. She came to see me and when her daughter phoned and asked me to come down here she offered to stay."

"Why was she there, and why did her daughter want to see you?"

"It was a personal matter."

"There's nothing personal in a murder enquiry, Miss Howard. You may as well tell me. It will come out ultimately."

"It's rather a long story and I don't think you'll believe me," I said wearily. "On Tuesday morning Betty tried to frame me on a shop-lifting charge. Fortunately, someone saw what she did, a man called Lee Dexter. He recognized Betty this morning and we were going to go to the police. Mrs. Singer came to beg me

149

not to go. Presumably her daughter wanted to ask the same thing."

"Why didn't you go to the police right away?"

"I'd decided against it."

"Why?"

It was no use bringing Ken into it. I knew that without even thinking about it. "I decided it was a pretty pointless thing to do."

"Are you sure that was your reason? You weren't afraid of what Miss Singer would reveal if you brought the police into it?"

"You've been listening to gossip already, Inspector!"

"No. It was a reasonable assumption to make. I think that will be all for the moment, Miss Howard."

"All?"

"For the moment," he repeated.

"Oh I see," I said bitterly. "You're going to do some checking before you start again."

"That's right. I'll get a car to take you home and bring Mrs. Singer back here. Mr. Walton —I'd like you to remain for a few more minutes. Oh and Miss Howard, perhaps you'd allow the sergeant to take your fingerprints before you go."

They both rose as I got to my feet. Mr. Walton tried to give me a smile but it wavered and didn't quite come off.

The sergeant took me into the other room where a man was dusting the furniture with grey powder. He broke off and made a record of my fingerprints without an unnecessary word being spoken and then the sergeant ushered me out to the police car parked outside.

A crowd had gathered in the street. The people stared at me, heedless of the rain, their faces pale and anonymous but common in their avid curiosity. "That's Nell Howard," I heard someone say and another echoed the cry and added, "She did it. Killed poor Betty. Never gave her a chance—"

I was glad when the car whisked me away from the rising murmurs. Lynching might not be common in the United Kingdom but I had an uneasy feeling that left to push my own way through that crowd I wouldn't have emerged with a whole skin.

The sergeant stayed with me, taciturn and self-effacing. I let him break the news to Mrs. Singer and stayed out of the way until they had gone.

It seemed odd to have to think about Ken's

dinner as if nothing had happened. He got in at his usual time. I didn't tell him anything. I'd not said anything the night before either. He'd come home then but gone out immediately after he'd eaten.

Tonight he seemed disposed to stay in. I cleared up after the meal and joined Chrissie in a game of snap until it was her bedtime.

Ken had the television on but I didn't think he was actually watching it. He hated quiz programmes of any description and sat through one without a murmur.

I picked up a book wondering how long it would be before the police came to ask more questions. They worked through the night. It could be any time. It could be when Ken was there. I didn't want that. I couldn't bear to think of him, sitting there, smirking, glad that I was in trouble. He knew something. His behaviour gave that away. But not one word did he say about it all night long. It was a strange evening; we were both engrossed in our thoughts.

The police came when he'd gone the next morning. I was having a cup of coffee. My tenth of the morning.

Egan and his taciturn sergeant, notebook at the ready again.

They refused my offer of coffee. Egan looked tireder than ever. His eyes were shadowed and he chose a hardbacked chair as if afraid the upholstered armchairs might lull him into slumber.

The first thing he did was to produce a knife and ask me if I recognized it.

I shook my head. It was a vegetable knife with a slender little blade, a type to be found in most kitchens. I used one myself. "It's not the sort of thing you carve your initials on," I said. "How could I recognize it? There must be millions like it."

"You have one yourself?"

"Yes."

"Would you mind showing it to us."

He didn't believe I could produce it. I could see it on his face.

I went into the kitchen and pulled open the cutlery drawer. I was a fool to expect it to be in its usual place. I realized that as I turned the knives over with my finger. My handkerchief . . . now the knife. Would it have my fingerprints on it? Mine or Chrissie's depending on who had wiped up the last time it was used.

When was that? Tuesday. The carrots . . .
Mrs. Singer slicing the top of her finger with
that very knife.

I tried to remember beyond that and
couldn't. I saw only the blood dripping from
her finger. Such a lot of blood and yet there
had been hardly any on Betty.

"It's not there?"

I jumped. Egan had come up behind me. For
a moment I was tempted to pick up another
knife, slightly bigger but sufficiently like it to
pass it off but my courage failed me. I thought
of being found out. Caught in one lie might
prove fatal, for me.

"It doesn't seem to be."

He turned the knives over picking up the one
I'd had my eye on. "This isn't it?"

I hesitated again and then said reluctantly,
"No, that's bigger. I use that one for cubing
stewing steak."

"A temptation, Miss Howard?" Egan smiled
faintly. "But a weakness to lie. You see if your
knife had been here it would have been very
hard to explain away your fingerprints on the
murder weapon."

That was something I'd not thought of. My
fingers slipped on the drawer as I closed it. I

had so nearly fallen into that trap—if a trap it was.

I raised my eyes. "What else have you found out?"

"A great many things." He moved back into the living-room.

"There has been ill-feeling between you and the dead girl for a long time and about a dozen people have come forward to tell me that you attacked Betty with a knife only last Saturday."

"It wasn't like that. She made me mad and I snatched up the first thing that came to hand. I didn't touch her."

"Because you were stopped." He motioned me to sit down. "What did Betty say when she telephoned?"

"She didn't speak to me—only to ask for her mother."

"So it was Mrs. Singer who sent you down there?"

"Well, yes . . . but it wasn't her idea. I'm sure of it."

I stared at him, trying to read what was on his mind. He surely couldn't believe Mrs. Singer had sent me to see her daughter without her knowledge. Why should she do such a thing? It would only have led to another slanging match between us. And it had been Betty on the phone. There had been no mistaking her voice. She had been alive when her mother had been at the house with me.

"Why did you go to see her?" Egan said abruptly.

"I felt sorry for Mrs. Singer. She begged me to go."

"But there wasn't much point, was there? Why didn't you simply tell her you'd decided not to go to the police?"

I looked down at my hands. "I suppose I felt it was throwing away an advantage."

"You enjoyed the feeling of power it gave you?"

"It wasn't like that," I said with an edge to my voice. "I knew Betty. A troublemaker of the first water. It would have been stupid to have told her I wasn't going to the police. She'd have thought I was afraid of her."

"But she would have realized you weren't going before very much time had elapsed."

"Yes . . ." I agreed reluctantly. "Let's say then that I wanted her to suffer as long as possible."

"Is that a fact?"

"I just said so, didn't I?" I said tartly. He

didn't sound as if he believed me. And it was true. Well, nearly . . .

"I'll tell you something, Miss Howard. I'm far more interested in what you are not saying. What are you afraid of?"

"Nothing."

"Not even of being charged with murder?"

"I credit you with more intelligence than the thug who got hold of me in the house."

"I've read his report."

"Naturally. Did he say I attacked him? Resisting arrest? He's a fool but no doubt he knows enough to be able to cover himself."

"He made an understandable mistake. Someone had phoned in and said a fight was going on. You were even named. The fear was expressed that you were trying to kill her . . . again."

"Who made that call?"

"We've been trying to trace her."

"A woman?"

"Female at least."

"And it wasn't a neighbour? No." I could see it wasn't. They'd have asked them first. "I suppose it hasn't occurred to you that Betty made the call herself and staged the whole thing. I'd have walked in and she'd have started a fight so that the police would haul me away for assault. It would be my word against hers, wouldn't it? Maybe she intended to offer to drop the charge if I kept quiet about the other thing."

"Is that what happened? And you were so infuriated you killed her?"

"I didn't kill her," I said flatly, but he went on as if I'd not spoken.

"I understand you have an extremely hot temper. Perhaps you didn't realize what you were doing."

"Trying to give me a way out, Inspector? Does that make it manslaughter instead of murder? No." I met his eyes bleakly. "I didn't have time to kill her."

"It was fortunate you met Mr. Walton, wasn't it?"

"Are you trying to say it wasn't a chance meeting?"

"It's possible. You could have gone down there, found out what she was planning and killed her in a fit of rage. Then you could have doubled back on your tracks and picked the vicar as an eminently suitable witness to vouch for you."

"Wouldn't I have made sure he came into the house with me if that were the case?"

"Perhaps you wanted a few seconds alone to check that you hadn't left any incriminating evidence behind."

"Such as my handkerchief? But it wasn't until the vicar had gone to phone the police that I noticed that."

"Why should she be clutching your handkerchief?"

"Someone knew I was on the way obviously."

"Yes . . . Whom do you have in mind?"

I stood up abruptly. Ken, of course. But what good would it do to hurl wild accusations around? For wild it would seem to anyone else.

"It's in your own interests to tell us everything, Miss Howard," Egan said, expressionlessly. "Things look very bad for you and I know you are holding something back."

I glanced at the sergeant, his pencil poised over the notebook. His face was a mask of indifference. I didn't think anything I said would surprise him.

"You won't believe me," I said. "I've no proof. I just feel my stepfather had something to do with it. Betty let something slip that seemed to indicate he had put her up to my

159

getting picked up for shoplifting. He had been the one to arrange I was in the store that morning. He wanted me to buy some perfume. Mrs. Singer knew about it although she denies my stepfather was involved. She's afraid of him. Betty was afraid of him too but I think she went running to him when I threatened to go to the police. And I think he suggested this way of keeping me quiet. She'd have fallen for it. It would have appealed to her. She wouldn't have seen that she was a danger to him and was better out of the way once and for all. He couldn't afford to have his good name smeared and it must have been obvious she couldn't withstand any kind of pressure. Killing her and getting me blamed for it was killing two birds with one stone."

His expression hadn't changed by as much as a blink. I expected some comment, even one that poured scorn and disbelief over my theory, but there was nothing. He waited as if expecting more.

"Don't you see that that's how it must have been?" I said despairingly. "Who else had access to my room, to this house? Who else would have bothered to involve me? He wants me out of the way."

"Why?" The question was flat and bored, perfunctory even, as if he felt he had to say something just for the record.

"I told you you wouldn't believe me," I snapped. "It was a waste of time telling you, wasn't it? And now you'll tell him and put him on his guard and he'll do something horrible."

He disregarded all that and said, "Answer my question. Why should he want you out of the way? Could it be that you're a rich heiress and your wicked guardian wants you out of the way so he can claim your inheritance?"

I took a deep breath and sat down again. He was trying to get me angry, to see for himself just how hot-tempered I was. He couldn't know anything about my father. Or could he? Had he talked to Lee?

"I don't think the fact of my inheritance has anything to do with it," I said deliberately. "Ken would gain nothing whatever happened to me."

He blinked then. So he hadn't known. He *was* just trying to rile me.

"I've no time for fairy tales," he said curtly.

"Neither have I. Or sarcasm either. If you're going to charge me, get it over and done with.

I'm not going to waste more of my breath telling you things you so obviously disbelieve."

"What's this about an inheritance?"

"I don't wish to discuss it with you. Find out instead where my stepfather gets all his money from. He's got a safe in there packed with bank notes. He's also got a gun. Does he have a licence for it? You could find that out without too much trouble, couldn't you?"

"What sort of gun?"

"I didn't examine it thoroughly. Something else you won't believe; I was so frightened at the sight of it I couldn't get out of the room quick enough. Does a murderess act like that? But of course it's different when you're in a red hot rage. I could do anything then."

"Where is this gun?"

"In there." I jerked my head towards the den. "But you can't check up on my story. It's locked and Ken has the only key."

He got up and went over to the door. "Someone's tried to force this."

"Yes. We had a burglary. They didn't take anything though." Or maybe they did. Was that when the knife and my handkerchief were taken? I paused at the thought. It needn't be Ken then. But who else could want me out of the way? And who else could have wanted Betty dead?

"The police were informed," I went on slowly. "Ken wasn't very pleased with me for doing that either."

"When was this?"

I had to consider. So many things had happened it was hard to work out the days. "Monday I think. Yes, it was Monday. The Bank Holiday."

"How did they get in?"

"Oh that was easy enough. The window was smashed the night before."

"How?"

I met his eyes without a flicker. "Someone threw a brick through the window. Ken wouldn't let me tell the police about that. He acted as if he were afraid someone was trying to kill *him*. If you ask me he's a blackmailer —but I'm wasting my breath again, in saying something like that, aren't I? Before I know where I am I'll be facing a charge of slander on top of everything else."

"Does he know you hate him so much?"

"I imagine so. He works at keeping it fired."

"You've only been living here on a permanent basis since your mother died at Christmas. Is that right?"

"Yes."

"Has he ever made a pass at you?" He was prowling round the room, lifting first one thing then another to give it a cursory examination.

"No," I said shortly.

"Then what has he done to earn such hatred?"

"It would all seem very petty and childish to you and it's hardly relevant to your enquiry. Do you think I murdered Betty?"

"It's possible. Would you have any objection to our searching this house?"

"I wouldn't but Ken would."

"Taking my name in vain again, Nell," Ken said smoothly from the doorway. "What has she been saying to you, Inspector? It is Inspector, isn't it? I would expect no less for a murder enquiry. I'm Ken Manning, the owner of this house."

Egan introduced himself and the sergeant and explained he'd just been asking for permission to search the house.

"So you've no search warrant?" Ken said raising his eyebrows. "It's not as serious as I was led to believe then?"

"I beg your pardon?" Egan was austere and slightly remote.

Ken blinked his baby blue eyes at him. "I understand it's all round the town that my step-daughter murdered poor Betty Singer. I found it incredible to believe—not so much that she had lost her temper once again—but that she could remain silent about the whole thing. Do you know she never said one word to me last night. She never even attempted to broach the subject." He shook his head sorrowfully. "A strange child. I've never understood her. Indulged of course in her early years. It's always a mistake."

"You were going to search the house," I said pointedly to Egan.

"Of course, of course," Ken said affably. "Go right ahead."

"Would you open this door."

"Of my den?" He glanced at me. "Now I *know* she's been talking about me. Well, you'll find nothing here, Inspector. I'm afraid this locked door has always intrigued her. She used to imagine all sorts of things were behind it, from a hoard of treasure to a sort of Bluebeard's cupboard." He unlocked the door and threw it open. "As you can see I use it both as an office and a refuge. Children being so inquisitive and destructive I found it necessary to keep the door locked. Even so, this one here did her best to get in. You'll see the marks on the door."

"That wasn't me."

He ignored me, giving Egan a humorous glance and shrug as if to say a denial was to be expected but not believed.

"One doesn't usually find such large safes in a private house," Egan commented. He wasn't prowling around this room. He stood perfectly still and let his eyes do the wandering.

"You want to see inside that too?" Ken was all eagerness to oblige. "I've got absolutely nothing to hide."

Of course he didn't. I should have known. He would have got rid of anything incriminating knowing the police would be calling on me.

"It's a large safe," he explained, "because there are times when I have a considerable amount of money on hand. I'm a bookmaker—not that I advertise that fact here in Carsdale. I'm not ashamed of it but it's hardly a gentleman's profession." He pulled open the door of the safe and stood back. All those stacks of notes had gone. He couldn't resist smiling at me. Egan caught it but his face betrayed nothing. He went on his knees in front of the safe.

"You'll find my wife's jewellery," Ken said, "and a few odds and ends."

"You have a gun," Egan said, making a statement of it. He turned over the things in the safe and then stood up slowly and went over to the cabinet.

"Dear me, no," Ken exclaimed. "Where did you get such an idea?"

Egan didn't tell him. He pulled open the drawers of the cabinet. It wasn't locked and the folders had gone. In their place was what looked like a collection of catalogues. The lower drawers were empty.

"You had files in there," I burst out. "With people's names on them—and there were tapes in the bottom drawer."

"Now how would you know that?" Ken said silkily.

"I was in here and you know it. You were worried about what I might have seen. That's why you put Betty up to framing me. You were afraid I might tell someone—and a convicted shoplifter wouldn't stand a good chance of being believed."

Ken shook his head and lifted his hands up in a display of sorrow to the Inspector. "She's always been the same," he said sadly. "Full of delusions, almost paranoic. She drove her poor mother to an early grave."

"You rotten liar," I said in a low voice. "You're the one who killed her. And you killed Betty too."

"Where were you yesterday afternoon, Mr. Manning?" Egan said smoothly.

"You're surely not taking any notice of these wild accusations. I was at work of course. My clerks will vouch for me."

"And were you at work the day before?" I demanded.

"Where else would I be?"

"We saw you—at Winters Hall."

"Winters Hall . . . Winters Hall," he said musingly. "Ah yes. That place you were mooning about. That's another thing, Inspector. Imagine this. She believes she's related to the people there because she shares the same name. Next thing you know she'll be saying she's the lost daughter of the house, sold to the gypsies when she was a baby or some such tale. Don't laugh at her. Betty made that mistake."

"You might pull the wool over the Inspector's eyes about a lot of things," I said hotly. "But I happen to have met my father and talked to him."

"Your father!" Ken said pityingly. "Don't be such a little idiot. He was dead before you were born."

"He wants to see you," I said steadily. "At Winters Hall on Saturday."

"Tomorrow?"

It was Friday already? I couldn't believe it. And Lee had said he'd phone.

"Yes," I said slowly.

"You've left it a little late, haven't you?"

"I wasn't going to tell you at all. I knew what your reaction would be."

"Naturally. I'm not taken in by your fantasies any longer."

"Why don't you phone him?"

"I'll do that. I'll put an end to this once and for all." He strode over to the phone and asked the operator for the number of the Howard family at Winters Hall, writing it down as she reeled it off.

There was no premonition in me this time. I smiled at the triumph in his eyes as he started to dial the number.

He covered the mouthpiece and looked at Egan. "Her mother humoured her in these kind of things. I always knew it was a mistake. Oh hello." He moved his hand. "I'd like to speak to Mr. Howard please. Mr. George Terence Howard . . . What?" He beckoned me over. "Would you repeat that, please?"

He held the receiver up to my ear and I heard a man's voice say, "There's no one of that name here."

"That is Winters Hall, isn't it?" I demanded.

"Yes, it is."

"But Mr. Howard lives there. He owns the Hall."

"I'm afraid you've got the wrong number." The clunk of the receiver sounded very loud in my ears.

Ken took the receiver from me. His smile nearly split his face in two. "So he wants to see me," he said with heavy sarcasm. "A dead man wants to see me."

I could only stare at him. Had some kind of macabre joke been played on me? Wasn't he my father after all? But then who was he? And why make such a claim? But it was Lee who had told me. Lee again.

7

I PICKED up the phone again. I wasn't going to accept it at that.

First I checked the number with the operator but Ken hadn't cheated. The same man came on the line. "Mr. Lee Dexter please," I said crisply.

"One moment."

It was more than one moment and it felt like a million years. Egan had his eyes on me. I thought I detected some sympathy in them and it was far more mortifying than any disbelief.

Ken was openly gloating. "What do you hope to achieve now?"

I ignored him and then Lee's lazy Texan drawl came on the line and I tumbled unsteadily into speech. "It's Elinor, I asked for my father and was told no one of that name was there."

"Oh, I'm sorry, Elinor. I should have given you his number. It's unlisted. Got a pencil handy?"

"Yes."

He told me the number and I wrote it down.

"Why couldn't the man who answered have told me that?"

"There isn't much point in having an unlisted number if you hand it out to anyone who rings up. I don't suppose you mentioned who you were, did you?"

"No. But he seemed to deny my father's existence."

"And you can guess why, can't you? Your father has very little contact with the outside world and woe betide anyone who intrudes without good reason. It was six weeks before I saw him and I had stayed here a month before I knew of his existence. Anyway, how are you? Have you talked it over with your stepfather?"

"Not exactly." I paused. It was difficult to sort out what to say next. "The fact is I'm in trouble. Betty—the girl in the newsagents we saw yesterday morning—was murdered in the afternoon and I'm the prime suspect. The police are here now. Ken has just about convinced them I'm paranoic, suffering from delusions, given to fantasies and lord knows what else." I could hear my voice shaking and thinning out. "When that man said no one of my father's name was there it was like a horrible nightmare."

Lee's voice was reassuringly firm and confident. "Put them on. Don't worry."

"You don't understand. She's dead. It's murder. And everyone thinks I did it."

"Let me speak to the man in charge and then I'll be right over. Don't worry." He spoke soothingly as if I were an infant child to be mollified. It had the reverse effect naturally. I didn't think he took me seriously.

I sniffed and held out the phone to Egan. "He wants to speak to you."

"Who's Lee Dexter?" Ken said nastily as Egan spoke into the phone.

"A friend of my father's."

"Of your father's," he said scornfully. "I made enquiries. You can't fool me. He's dead all right."

"Maybe you didn't ask the right people. Why were you at the Hall?"

"Never you mind. I'll tell you this though—if your father is still alive he's got some explaining to do."

"Not to you, Ken."

"Oh no? Who's the one who's been saddled with you all these years? You've had the best of everything and what have I had in return? Nothing but ingratitude. Now this—lie upon lie. You stole my keys, didn't you? You opened the safe, you went through my desk."

"I was only looking for my birth certificate. And how did you know I'd been through your desk? Because the gun was there?"

"There was no gun."

"Oh yes there was. And there were files too. I even remember some of the names."

"What were they, Miss Howard?"

I jumped. I'd forgotten Sergeant Turpin sitting quietly back in his corner. I think Ken had forgotten too but he didn't lose his composure.

"Go on," he smiled. "What were they?"

I stared at him. He was so confident. Did he think they'd be too scared to admit they were being blackmailed?

"They were in alphabetical order," I said slowly. "The first was Armstrong. Janine Armstrong I think." I closed my eyes, visualizing the neat entries in their perspex slots. I managed about ten names but Ken's smile didn't falter. "She's made them up," he said. "Oh you'll probably find people of those names —they're common enough after all—but they won't know me or anything about me."

"I'd recognize one of them," I said slowly.

"I pulled the file out. Edward Rigby. There was a photograph in it—a couple having dinner somewhere. I think I'd know the girl. She was very striking, rather like Elizabeth Taylor."

Ken's smile faltered then but only for a moment. Egan came off the phone and he turned to him. "Well? Is her father alive?"

"It would appear so." He glanced down at something he'd written on a sheet from the telephone pad and put it away carefully in his inner breast pocket. "We'll be on our way."

"But you haven't finished searching the house," I protested.

"I think it's a waste of effort. Don't you, Miss Howard?"

I wasn't quite sure how I was meant to take that. In fact I didn't know exactly what to make of Egan at all.

He said, "We'll see you again," and with his silent shadow on his heels he left the house. A promise or a threat? His tone left me guessing.

Ken's smile left his face as though wiped off with a sponge. "Now what did you tell them?" he demanded.

"Wouldn't you like to know!"

"You'll tell me, my little lady, and you'll learn a lesson you won't forget in a hurry. I won't have anyone interfering in my business. Where's Chrissie?"

"She's not here."

"Get her."

I didn't move although my stomach felt it had taken an express lift to my toes. "I'll do no such thing."

"I'm going to tell her what you did to poor Betty, tell her that you're going to be locked up, tell her that she won't be seeing you any more." He was beginning to smile again. He was in his element once more, achieving the effect he wanted.

I wanted to kill him. I could feel violent urge throbbing through my whole body. I felt I'd burst with the effort of restraining it.

"I suppose she'll be next door." He walked across the floor and pulled the door open just as the bell rang.

"Oh, I was—Oh Ken!" It was Mrs. Singer. She sounded on the verge of hysteria. "I saw the police car. What happened? Why haven't they arrested her? Where is she?"

Ken dropped his voice. I couldn't have heard even if I'd wanted to but I was backing away into the kitchen and then out through the back door into the garden and climbing the fence over into the Jennings' with only a brief pause to pick up my handbag. There was no sign of Chrissie and Libby in the garden, even Mr. Jennings was not in evidence.

I knocked on their door and Mrs. Jennings answered. Her smile was a little strained. So Ken hadn't been lying about the way people were talking. She called for Chrissie without asking me inside and Chrissie came running, a daub of paint on her face and her hands streaked with vivid colours.

"Get your coat, Chrissie," I said.

"But we're in the middle of something. We're painting! It's not lunchtime yet, is it?"

"Come along."

She looked startled at the sharpness of my tone.

"Hurry," I added with a glance behind me.

"Well, all right." She got her coat but her movements were slow and reluctant.

I went to the corner of the house and cautiously peered round the corner to our front door.

Ken had taken Mrs. Singer inside. They wouldn't see us now unless they were at the window.

"Where are we going?" Chrissie demanded, coming up to me with dragging feet.

"I don't know. Let's run." I took her hand and pulled. Where could we go? I had very little money. Getting away from Ken. That was the main thing. Before he shattered Chrissie's fragile world. If I knew him he'd hit out as cruelly as he could without a thought for anything but teaching me a lesson. I didn't think it would make any difference whether I told him what I'd said to the police or not. He'd tell Chrissie either way, just for the pleasure of seeing my agony of mind.

"Why are we running?" Chrissie panted. "And you've got no coat. What's the matter?"

"I'll explain later." I was glad we lived at the top of a hill. Lack of a coat didn't matter. I was generating heat.

Mr. Walton! He'd look after Chrissie for a little while. I'd go back to the house. Lee had said he'd come. He could take us somewhere. I wondered what he'd said to Egan, whether Egan would do anything about Ken.

I had to slow to a walk. I had a crippling stitch. "I'm going to take you to Mr. Walton," I said gaspingly. "I want you to stay there until I come back for you."

178

"Are we running away?"

"Yes."

"From my father?"

"Yes."

"He'll find us and bring us back," she said, considering the matter with a seriousness that belied her age.

"Maybe he won't have much time to look for us." I hesitated. I had to prepare her in some way—just in case. "Chrissie . . . I want you to believe in me. If you hear anything bad about me remember that I love you and wouldn't do anything to hurt you."

"What's the matter, Nell?"

"People are saying I've done a wicked thing and your father is trying to make everyone believe it."

I pushed open the gate into the cemetery. It would be wiser to enter the vicarage by the back way.

"I don't like my father," Chrissie said slowly. "He frightens me. Mr. Jennings isn't like him one bit. He plays with Libby—and he's kind and good."

"Yes, darling. I know." I threaded through the graves wondering what to say to Mr. Walton. He wouldn't understand. No one would understand. They'd put me in the wrong. Perhaps say I was kidnapping the child even. And for what? Because I was afraid of her learning the truth about me. For a moment I wished Ken had sometimes descended to physical cruelty. People understood cuts and bruises. They would never appreciate what a man like Ken could do to a child without lifting a finger. The scars he left would only be apparent when she was older and even then they wouldn't be attributed to him.

The housekeeper answered my knock and when I asked for Mr. Walton led us into the parlour, looking at both of us in concern. "I'll get you some tea," she said. "I don't think he'll be long. Is something wrong?"

"No—Yes. That is . . . would you say we're not here if anyone should ask?"

"They're making trouble, are they?" Her face darkened. "I've seen it happen before and no doubt I'll see it again. People like to believe the worst about everyone but themselves. Mr. Walton has done his best but they don't want to listen to anything that denies them the thrill of running someone into the ground, especially someone who— Well, never mind. You'll be safe here." She smiled at Chrissie. "Maybe you'd like some hot scones? I've only just taken them out of the oven." She cocked her head. "There's the vicar now. You come with me, Chrissie. No doubt your sister wants a private word with him."

I smiled at her gratefully and went out to meet the vicar.

He was taking off his coat in the hall, the stoop of his shoulders very pronounced. In the moment before he saw me I thought how unutterably weary he looked. His demeanour was that of a man defeated on all counts. But then he saw me and he straightened up as well as he was able, light and fire returning to his eyes. "Elinor! I meant to call on you."

"I'm here to beg sanctuary," I said as lightly as I could. "For Chrissie. I want to take her away for a little while."

"Yes . . . It's understandable I suppose. She knows nothing yet?"

"No."

He moved into his study, his head bowed, his brow clouded, and he sat down carefully, easing himself into the chair as if his joints were giving him pain.

"She can stay here as long as you feel it necessary," he said.

"It will only be for an hour or two."

"And then what?"

"I thought we might go to a hotel in Manchester."

"What does your stepfather say?"

"I'm going back now to tell him."

"What's happened, Elinor? You're as white as a sheet."

"We've been running. I'm not used to it."

"You've no coat! Wasn't there time to pick it up?"

He saw too much—always he saw too much. There was no getting away from it. "Ken was going to tell Chrissie," I said in a low voice. "He was going to tell her I'd killed Betty and was going to be locked up; that she'd never see me again."

"Aren't you exaggerating, Elinor? He probably felt it better she be told by him than by an outsider. Have you been in the town this morning?"

"No."

"The talk is of nothing else. She is bound to find out before long."

"I don't want her to find out from Ken."

"Then tell her yourself."

"Not yet. The police might find out who did it before long. Someone must have seen him."

"Him?"

"Ken!"

The vicar closed his eyes. When he spoke his voice was thin and weary. "You must stop this. You do yourself no good."

"He killed her. I know he did," I said passionately.

The housekeeper came in with a tea tray. She had heard me. Her expression was startled and shocked but she put the tray down without a word and departed without attempting to linger.

"People are saying the same thing about you with even more conviction," the vicar said tiredly. "Don't you see how wrong it is?"

"I don't care. All I want is to keep Chrissie out of his way. Will you help me or not?"

"You're going back to see your stepfather now?"

"Yes."

"I think it best that Chrissie goes away for a few days but he must agree, Elinor. I'll be party to nothing underhand. I'll want your assurance that he knows where you are going."

If I had to lie to the vicar, I would, without

a qualm, for Chrissie's sake. I said evenly, "Very well. I'll go back now and tell him I'm taking Chrissie away."

He made no attempt to rise as I left and I suspected the tea would go cold long before he roused himself. He probably guessed I'd lie. Probably? No. He'd know it. But he had to give me the benefit of the doubt. That was the way his mind worked.

I hurried back up the hill and was half-way home before I realized Ken would have no difficulty in guessing where I had taken Chrissie if I returned in so short a time.

It didn't seem advisable to go into town after what the vicar had reported but it was too cold to hang around outside.

I hesitated. I didn't want to miss Lee but it would be at least another hour before he arrived.

As I stood there I saw Mrs. Singer start down the hill. I put a tree between her line of vision and myself but I think if I'd walked towards her she wouldn't have seen me.

Her head was down and something in her walk reminded me of the vicar; the droop of the shoulders, the weary way she was carrying herself, even her jutting breasts had lost their bounce.

I stepped out from the shelter of the tree when she was about a yard away and she jumped violently as I greeted her. "Hello, Mrs. Singer."

"You!" she breathed.

I didn't know quite what I expected, what Ken had said to her, what she believed, but I was wholly unprepared for a tigerish attack. I went down on the ground as she launched herself forward, her nails raking at my face.

"Murderer! Murderer!" she screamed at the top of her voice.

I caught her wrists desperately and tried to heave her off me as she fought to free herself. The fall had winded me and her weight didn't help. I felt my skirt rip as I got my legs around her waist and tried to squeeze. She rolled on her side, in an attempt to crush my leg and break the hold, and I would have screamed if I'd had the breath to spare. For a moment I thought she'd broken it but somehow I contrived to swing and landed on top of her, my knees gripping in tightly at her side, maintaining my balance and helping me to sit firmly on her stomach.

I leaned forward, pressing her wrists down on the ground.

She tried to spit in my face, her eyes were glittering with insane madness.

"I didn't kill Betty," I gasped as she bumped and heaved beneath me. "You must know that."

"You liar! You liar!"

"I didn't. Don't you think the police would have arrested me if they thought I had? What did she say to you on the phone, Mrs. Singer? What did she tell you she was going to do?"

"Nothing! Nothing!"

"Did she ask you to phone the police? Giving me time to get to the house? I thought she might have done that herself but she couldn't very well, could she? The timing might not have been right. Then again Ken wouldn't have thought that a good idea. It would narrow his time for getting away."

"Ken?" She suddenly lay still.

"It was his idea, wasn't it? Another little frame up for me—only it wasn't so little after all. He had to kill Betty. She would have talked."

"Let me up."

"If you made that phone call from our house

186

the police will be able to check up on it." I spoke with more confidence than I felt but I saw at once it had gone home. Mrs. Singer had more faith in their powers than I. "Let me up," she said again but the power had gone from her voice.

I hesitated and then released my hold on her wrists and stood up.

She bounced to her feet and stood for a moment facing me. "You're a liar," she said, but it held none of the conviction of her previous assertion and she turned on her heel and started running down the hill.

I watched her, my hand going absently to my face. Both cheeks were bloodied and beginning to smart but I was far more interested in Mrs. Singer. What would she do now? Go to the police—or face Ken with what I'd said.

I felt a sudden uneasiness and glanced round. The houses on the hill were separated from the road by large gardens but someone could have witnessed that fight. If Mrs. Singer had any idea of facing Ken with what she knew and something happened to her it would be all round town that I'd done it again.

The nearest phone box was on the edge of town.

I set off in Mrs. Singer's wake and phoned the police, asking for Egan.

I was put through right away as soon as I'd given my name and I told him quickly what had happened. "She may be in danger," I said.

"And you're worried about her?"

"I just wouldn't like to have the blame put on my shoulders. I'm carrying enough of a load already. *Can* you check whether she made that phone call?"

"I'm afraid not."

"But she did make it, I'm sure she did."

"We'll talk to her."

And with that I had to be satisfied. I came out of the phone booth and glanced at my watch. It was almost one o'clock. Maybe Ken would have gone back to work. But his car was still outside.

I let myself in quietly by the back door. He was on the phone. I listened for a minute but it didn't make any sense to me and I crept upstairs and got my suitcase.

I'd almost filled it with Chrissie's clothes and was adding a few things of my own when I heard him coming up the stairs.

I grabbed a handful of underclothes at

random and jammed them in the case, throwing in my hairbrush and make-up on the top.

I was locking the case when he appeared in the doorway. "Where do you think you're going?"

"Anywhere so long as I'm not in your vicinity."

"That's what you think. Where's Chrissie?"

"Where you won't find her."

"Think not? You can unpack that case. You're not leaving here."

In answer to that I picked up the case and marched to the door. "Get out of my way."

He didn't seem to move. There was just a slight change in his stance and then his bunched fist landed on my jaw with such force that it lifted me clean off my feet and I went sprawling backwards across the floor.

"I'm tired of you," he said unpleasantly. "I'm tired of your high and mighty ways, tired of your ladylike manners and the way you look as if I'm something that's crawled out from under a stone. I broke your mother without lifting a finger. I'm admitting defeat by giving way to it now but by all that's holy you're going to change your attitude to me."

He raised his foot and kicked me viciously in

the side and then he hauled me up and flung me across the bed.

I was only half conscious. I couldn't even fight back as he slapped my face from side to side, the stinging blows setting my ears buzzing.

"Who've you been fighting with?" he said. "Who marked you?"

"Find out," I mumbled.

"Who?" He whipped my arm up behind my back, turning me over on the bed as easily as if I'd been a child.

"Who?"

I could feel the sweat break out on my brow. He was breaking my arm. "Mrs. Singer," I screamed.

The pressure didn't relax. "And where's Chrissie?"

"In the waiting-room at the station."

He released my arm and I sobbed with relief at the cessation of pain, despising myself for the weakness but unable to prevent it.

"I wouldn't bother telling anyone about this," Ken said in my ear. "They'll only believe you're making hay out of the few bruises you got from Mrs. Singer and I think it only fair to tell you that I know ways of making you crawl in agony that won't leave a mark on your body. Unless you want a sample I'd advise you to behave yourself in future and treat me with respect."

I didn't say anything and he jerked me over so that I was flat on my back once more. "I've just been offered five thousand pounds for getting rid of you," he remarked conversationally. "A little accident, the details to be left to me. I was tempted, I admit it. But what's five thousand compared to a steady income for life? We're going to live in style, you, me and Chrissie—that is if you're not arrested. I really am rather grateful to Mr. Walton after all. It wouldn't suit me to have you put away for a long sentence. Your father will have to show his gratitude for the way I've looked after you all these years. He's a rich man I believe—and you'll get it all if you play your cards right. Cat got your tongue?"

I was goaded into speech, despite every bruised nerve telling me to keep quiet. "The police will catch up with you. You'll be the one that's arrested."

"I think not. Proof is a requisite in dear old England and that they'll never get. I'm a careful man. Remember that—I always have been and I always will."

"You did kill Betty, didn't you?"

"Of course. She phoned me in a rare old state telling me you'd turned up with a witness who could identify her to the police. She actually threatened me. Me! No one does that. Oh, I could have laughed her story to scorn but it seemed advisable to get rid. It's funny how things work out. A couple of hundred I was offered. Fair enough I thought. For nuisance value—for making sure you didn't cause a scandal. But I wasn't told your father was still alive. To think I had my hands on a potential gold mine and nearly threw it away."

"What are you planning to do?" I whispered.

"Not to murder you. You needn't be afraid of that. We'll move in with your father at Winters Hall. You'll like that, won't you? And so will Chrissie. All you have to do is behave yourself and I'll look after you both."

"Who offered you the money to get rid of me?"

"Ah . . . I'm not telling you everything. You're going to need me . . . you can see that, can't you? Protection—that's what I'm offering.

Look at it sensibly and stop behaving like a silly child."

I closed my eyes. He was serious. He actually thought I could go along with him.

"What are you going to do about Mrs. Singer?"

"She won't say anything to the police. She's scared to death of me, besides which she made the mistake of telling me one or two things about her past that could land her in trouble. She thinks you killed Betty anyway. She thinks you really did have a fight. Silly old fool." He changed tone abruptly. "I'll get Chrissie. Clean yourself up and make yourself presentable. There's no need for her to know anything is wrong now."

I dragged myself off the bed and stood up. The pain in my side was the worst—it hurt when I breathed—but my jaw wasn't doing a bad job of throbbing; every tooth in my head felt as if it had been jolted out of its socket and was protesting about settling down again.

"*Are* you going to behave yourself?" Ken demanded.

"Yes," I said listlessly.

He thrust his face close to mine. "If you don't, I'll collect that five thousand as a bonus.

It suits me better to keep you alive but I'm not going to be dogmatic about it unless you cooperate."

"You might find your prospective victim unwilling to give you a life income."

"Don't worry about that. They always pay and go on and on. You did very well with those names by the way but even if they admitted they were being blackmailed they don't know who I am. That's what I mean by being careful."

"This one knows your name."

"Ah, but this one is different. We're going to live together. It will make it much more entertaining—poetic justice in fact. People should never try to cheat me. A measly two hundred to keep you quiet and out of the way. And only when I telephone and say your father already knows about you do I get a real offer. Well . . . enough of that. Which way is it going to be? A life of comfort or no life at all?"

"Do you call that a choice?"

He smiled. "I thought you might see it that way. And if you have any ideas of double crossing me, remember what I can do to you. I have no scruples—none at all. And there's always Chrissie. You wouldn't want anything . . . unpleasant to happen to her, would you?"

It was some minutes before I could move after he'd gone. I pulled on another skirt with difficulty and washed my face. A bruise was already beginning to appear on the point of my chin but it didn't look half as bad as it felt.

Ken would have reached the station by now. I had to hurry and get out of the house before he got back. How could he expect me to cooperate with him in any way at all? Could he really believe I would be so afraid of him and so afraid of the unknown person who wanted me dead that I would do what he wanted?

I picked up the suitcase, got my warmest coat and slipped out of the house. I couldn't go straight to Chrissie and risk Ken seeing me on his return from the abortive pick-up at the station. I had to find a hiding-place where I could see Lee arrive. The laurel bush was no good in the daylight. I went inside the garage, covered the case with an old sack and placed myself at the edge of the window. If Ken decided to drive in the garage I'd have plenty of time to slip out of the rear door as he lifted up the front but I didn't think he'd do that.

He'd be anticipating further use of the car that day and would leave it in the drive.

I pushed up my sleeve and couldn't believe it was nearly three o'clock. Lee should have arrived ages ago if he'd set out at once. Where was he?

I began to wonder if he had arrived whilst I was out and Ken had got rid of him when I heard a car coming and the yellow Capri slid to a standstill on the road outside.

I had taken two steps towards the door when I realized there were two cars. Ken had been right behind Lee. He cut his engine seconds after Lee had got out of the Capri. I pressed in against the wall by the window.

Lee was half-way up the path when Ken hurried after him. "I'm Ken Manning. Can I help you?"

Lee paused, appraising him thoughtfully. "I've come to see your stepdaughter."

"Oh, I'm sorry. I can't possibly allow that." Ken's voice was officious and brusque. "She's in bed, not very well at all. Who are you?"

"Lee Dexter."

"Oh yes." Ken's voice altered and became more conciliatory. "She phoned you this morning. You're a friend of her father's, I take it."

"That's right."

"What sort of man can abandon his own daughter and leave another man to bring her up?" He injected disgust and contempt in the question. One of his usual ploys in making himself out to be so good and charitable by running down someone else.

"I presume Elinor hasn't talked to you yet," Lee said slowly.

"Talk to me!" Ken laughed without humour. "Do the young these days ever talk to their parents? She's a difficult girl, very difficult. However, I mustn't bore you with my problems. I'd like to see this father of hers."

"Of course. He's expecting you tomorrow afternoon sometime. I must explain that he's something of a recluse. He suffered a great deal during the war."

"The war! It's been over nearly twenty years," Ken said scornfully.

"Yes, indeed," Lee said without expression. "But the scars remain."

"You mean . . ." Ken paused and then changed tactics. "You can appreciate this puts me in rather an awkward position."

"Indeed?" Lee said again. He made it sound flat and bleak.

"Why yes. There's my own daughter to consider." He called out. "Chrissie! Come on out of the car."

I stiffened in every limb. So he had guessed where I had taken her when he'd not found her at the station. Clever, clever Ken.

"Hello, Chrissie," Lee said warmly.

"Hello." She was shy and bashful.

Ken said, "So you two have met already— and not a word to me. I expect that sort of behaviour from Nell but not from my own daughter. You can see what a bad influence she is, Mr. Dexter. She needs a firm hand. Can her father provide that? She's been spoiled, indulged too much over the years. These last three months since her mother died have been the worst of my life. She resents any form of criticism and imagines she can do exactly as she wishes."

I could see what he was doing. I wondered if Lee could. But then he could have no idea of Ken's goal. He couldn't guess that he was preparing the way for a new home for the three of us. What would he suggest first; a visit to get to know each other? I couldn't see my father refusing that. He wouldn't know it for the thin edge of the wedge, the gradual easing in that Ken meant to make permanent. Ken would make him feel under an obligation, he would try to prove that I needed his controlling hand. He would play on my father's feelings, making him feel guilty over the bigamous marriage and Chrissie's illegitimacy. Oh there were a hundred and one ways which he could try on my father, honing and refining as he judged which would be the more effective.

I slumped against the side of the garage. Never in my life had I felt more helpless. If the police were unable to prove he had killed Betty he would be free to do just as he wanted. There was no way I could stop him. Who would believe me if I tried to repeat what he'd told me in my bedroom? And he had Chrissie. I couldn't run away now. I couldn't leave her with him—a self-confessed murderer.

8

I TOOK off my coat and put it with my bag under the sacking beside my case and then I wondered if I was doing the right thing. Once I was back inside the house Ken could make sure I stayed there—and he wouldn't trust me. Not after I had lied to him about Chrissie's whereabouts. Maybe it would be better if I stayed hidden. I might have a better chance of taking Chrissie away.

I went back to the window and risked a furtive glance. Ken was trying to get rid of Lee but Lee was refusing to take the hint. "I'd like to see Elinor," he said. "Even if it's only for a moment."

"She's had too many upsets today. I'm thinking of calling the doctor. She's talking very strangely, very strangely indeed. I'm worried about her. You know of course why the police have been here. Naturally I don't believe she could do such a thing but there's no denying she's in a very peculiar frame of mind." Ken put his hand on Lee's arm, urging him back towards the gate. "You can see her tomorrow —when she's more herself."

When he's had another go at me, I thought grimly. I must have jolted his confidence that he could make a puppet of me. Even with Chrissie in his hands he wasn't sure that I would restrain my tongue. Talking strangely indeed!

Lee resisted the pressure Ken was exerting and stood his ground. "I'll make allowances for what she's been through," he said, "but I must see her."

"Must!" Ken dropped his hand and glanced back at the house. They were standing side on now and Lee was facing me. I wondered if I could attract his attention without Ken knowing. He was obviously afraid I might come out of the house at any moment for he put his hands on Chrissie's shoulders as if to emphasize the hold he had. "What's so imperative about it that it can't wait twenty-four hours?"

"That's my business," Lee said with a mildness that was wholly deceptive.

I suddenly recognized that whatever he believed of Ken he was sufficiently concerned to make sure I was all right. And he wouldn't go until he'd seen me.

Ken was not so perceptive. The mild tone had fooled him.

"If you've any business with Nell I insist on knowing what it is. I'm her legal guardian and there's going to be no more underhand goings on. She's in enough trouble. Who are you anyway? A friend you say. What exactly does that mean?"

"I'm a friend of the Howard family and Elinor is part of that family." Lee's tone was measured and deliberate. "And as for your being her legal guardian I don't think the courts would uphold that, even if it were true."

"Are you a lawyer?"

"No."

"Then maybe you don't know that with Nell as old as she is her wishes will be taken into consideration."

"I'm anticipating that."

"I don't like your tone," Ken said waspishly. "Or your implication. She'll do as I say."

"Then why do you object to my seeing her?"

"I've her welfare at heart, that's why. She had a fight with the girl's mother, she's hysterical, she was hurt. She won't want anyone to see her the way she is."

"Nell's hurt?" Chrissie demanded in a small voice. "What do you mean? Where is she?"

"In the house. No." His grip tightened as she made to run from him. "She's lying down."

"I want to see her," Chrissie cried.

"That makes two of us," Lee said. "I'm afraid you'll have to face up to it, Mr. Manning, I'm not going until I've seen her."

Ken hesitated. I think for a moment he actually considered physical violence again but a few seconds appraisal of Lee's whipcord body made him decide it would not only be foolhardy but possibly humiliating as well.

He took a firm grasp of Chrissie's hand. "Very well then. You can have five minutes—no more. And I'll tell you right now, Mr. Dexter or whoever you are, if you've got any ideas about Nell you can forget them right now."

"Ideas?" Lee queried in a very soft voice.

"You know what I mean," Ken said belligerently. "From now on I'm going to keep a close watch on that girl. She'll have to learn that slyness doesn't pay."

He moved off up the path and Lee followed him. I had to make my mind up fast. If he started to look for me would he take Chrissie with him? I thought he would. Or take steps to make sure I couldn't get at her. He wouldn't touch me with Lee present but Lee wouldn't stay long and then both Chrissie and I would be exposed to whatever brand of cruelty he decided on to impress on us that running away didn't pay.

I stayed where I was but Ken didn't come rushing out. I wondered if I could get out of the garage and into the back of Lee's car but the path was too open. He would only have to glance out of the window.

Lee came out of the house after about a quarter of an hour but there was no opportunity of attracting his attention. Ken was with him and he walked as far as the gate as if to make sure he was off the premises and out of the way.

I heard Lee's car drive off and Ken went back to the house.

The tension was stringing out my nerves to an almost unbearable tension as I waited, wondering what he was doing inside the house, why he wasn't looking for me. Had he phoned the police? What had he said to Lee to explain my absence?

A low rumbling almost made me hit the

ceiling but it was only my stomach, objecting to the fact that lunchtime was long past.

Ken didn't come out to put away the car. Dusk started to fall and the street lights came on. Ken drew the curtains.

I'd put my coat back on when I decided my shivering was cold and not nerves but there was still a tendency to shiver in overwhelming waves and I started feeling sick with hunger. My side was aching where Ken had kicked me too. I wondered if he'd cracked a rib.

When it was really dark I slipped out of the garage and went round to the back of the house.

Lights were on in the dining-room and kitchen but Ken had drawn the curtains too well for me to see anything.

I went back to the garage, filled a pail with water from the tap outside and made half a dozen heart stopping trips to Ken's car until the tank was brim full. I wasn't sure it would have the same effect as sugar but I couldn't see it doing the car any good. Ken had to be stopped from following us.

Fairly pleased with my attempt at sabotage I started on the next phase.

We didn't have a ladder but Mr. Jennings did and I knew where he kept it.

I would never have believed that it could be so heavy—and awkward too. I had to give up the idea of carrying it and was reduced to moving one end along the ground and then the other and I wasn't helped by a first rate view of Mr. and Mrs. Jennings sitting watching television. They hadn't bothered to draw their curtains and it seemed impossible that they could be so oblivious of my presence when I could see them so clearly.

I reached the garden wall with only one setback when Mr. Jennings got up from his chair and left the room. I didn't move until he was back again and while I was crouched on the ground all sorts of things ran through my mind.

Maybe it would have been better to face Ken. What hope did I have of getting away with Chrissie and remaining hidden for long? If he'd not phoned the police already he was bound to do so when he found Chrissie was gone. I needed more money. Inevitably my mind leapt to all that booty which had been in the safe. He might have put it in the bank but somehow I doubted it. The bank kept records and any tax investigation would reveal it. No, he would have put it with those files and tapes—somewhere safe—where the police wouldn't think of looking.

The light sprang on in Chrissie's room and my head shot up. She was going to bed. It stayed on for about ten minutes and during that time Mr. Jennings came back and sat in his chair again.

I started hefting the ladder over the wall and into our garden and propped it up against the side of the house under Chrissie's window.

I'd never climbed a ladder before and it had never occurred to me that it could be dangerous, but looking down from what seemed an immense height and feeling as if a puff of wind might knock me or the ladder off balance, I decided it was a pastime I would leave strictly alone in future.

I tapped on Chrissie's window with my fingertips. I was afraid to call out in case Ken heard. She couldn't be asleep, not in so short a time. But she didn't come to the window.

I tapped again and risked saying her name just once in a low whisper. She could be frightened, lying petrified in her bed wondering who or what was trying to get in her bedroom.

The curtains were parted a bare inch and then were flung back.

I put my finger to my lips and pointed to the window, ducking my head as Chrissie thrust it open willy nilly. "Nell! What are you doing? Where have you been?"

The ladder seemed to slide a couple of inches, my heart did more than slide. I grabbed the window sill and hauled myself into the room.

"Get dressed," I whispered.

"All right." She switched on her bedside light but I promptly switched it off again. "We'll have to stay in the dark," I told her, still whispering. "Your father might see the light under the door."

"He was awful mad," Chrissie whispered back. "He shouted at Mr. Walton and then when he found you weren't here he shouted at Lee. He said he'd taken you away. He said all sorts of things. Lee was mad too but he didn't shout back. He just walked away."

"Never mind all that." I was groping for her clothes, helping her into them.

"Mr. Walton didn't want to let me go," Chrissie went on breathlessly. "He asked me an awful lot of questions when you'd gone and then when father came he took him into his study. I don't think he likes father any more. They were both awfully angry."

So Ken's control was slipping. It was a hopeful sign. If he so far forgot himself as to lose his temper with Mr. Walton he was in a bad way. He was generally so careful with him.

I groped under the bed for Chrissie's shoes. It wasn't so surprising really. After all, he'd committed a murder. However little conscience he had, it must be preying on his mind. He couldn't be as confident as he made out. He would be going over and over everything, checking and double-checking that he hadn't made a mistake that would bring the police down on him, and I must have jolted his confidence in himself, even if only a little.

"I'm ready," Chrissie whispered.

"Right. I'll go down first and you come out after me." I groped for the top of the ladder, preparatory to climbing out of the window and couldn't believe it when my hands met nothing but air.

I leaned out. I wasn't imagining things. The ladder had gone.

"What's the matter?" Chrissie whispered.

"The ladder's gone." It hadn't fallen. We'd have heard it.

My lips twisted in self contempt. Ken had

known I'd be back for Chrissie. He'd known all he had to do was wait.

I rushed for the door. I was going to lock it but Ken had beaten me to it. It was already locked on the other side and he must have been waiting to see the handle turn for I heard him laugh. "You'll stay there tonight," he said. "And I'll deal with you in the morning. I warned you. You can't say I didn't. Now think about what I'm going to do to you."

Chrissie had crept to my side. I put my arm round her and we clung to each other. "Do you hear me?" Ken said.

I didn't answer.

"I know you're there. I saw you with the ladder. I knew you'd try something."

I still didn't answer and he said threateningly, "Don't try anything else. I'm giving you one last chance—after that it will be the end of you."

The doorbell rang and he said, "I know who that is—no friend of yours I can tell you. You'd best keep quiet."

I looked through the keyhole but he'd taken the key with him. A second later the landing light went off.

Chrissie was shivering. "What are we going to do?"

"We'll tie the sheets together," I said practically. He wasn't going to beat me now. "Come on—let's hurry."

"Can I turn the light on now?"

"No, I don't think so." If Ken meant who I thought he meant it would be better not to advertise our presence. He might take matters into his own hands and save himself a whole lot of money.

I pulled the blankets from Chrissie's bed and knotted the two sheets together making a loop at one end. It didn't seem very long. I tried to add one of the blankets but couldn't get it to knot securely.

Whoever Ken's visitor was they were being very quiet. I pulled the chair over to the window and started to unhook one of the curtains. My fingers were clumsy, I was trying too hard, wrenching instead of being careful. Chrissie was quicker. As soon as she realized what I was doing she went to the other one, her nimble fingers unhooking it before I was threequarters of the way through mine.

I needed both. The knots seemed to use up half the length but I was so terrified of them slipping and Chrissie falling to the ground that I played it safe.

"Who's going first?" Chrissie asked. She was frightened and trying not to show it.

"I'll lower you down," I said. "You sit in that loop and hold on tight. I won't let you fall."

"But who's going to hold it for you?"

"I'll tie it round something." What I didn't know. The bed was a divan, there was nothing to take the sheets on that.

I switched on the light for a moment. I knew that room as well as I knew my own but never having examined it in the light of using it for an escape I couldn't think what the possibilities were.

A chest of drawers, a little dressing-table, a wardrobe, a bookshelf. Nothing with handy legs, nothing that would hold my weight. It would have to be one of the chairs, wedged across the window.

Chrissie's face was as white as chalk, her eyes as huge as saucers.

I switched the light off quickly. "You're going to be all right," I said, trying to be as calm and matter of fact as possible. It was hard with my pulse beat going like the clappers and

212

my heart hammering against my ribs but Chrissie wouldn't notice that.

I tied the sheet round my waist and put the looped end over Chrissie's head, helping her over the window ledge.

As I took her weight, my whole body seemed to stiffen with the strain. She weighed a whole lot more than the ladder. I gritted my teeth and braced a foot against the wall, paying the sheets out a little at a time. The worst moment was when one of the knots stuck over the window ledge and I had to work it over. I thought Chrissie's weight was going to swing me over and out too as I freed the sheet and I slammed into the wall, my breath coming out like a wheezing steam engine.

The cessation of strain on my shoulders and arms was like a release from torture on the rack. I looked out of the window and saw her hand come up in the darkness. She had made it.

I hauled the sheets up and undid the loop, tying it round the chair.

I wasn't looking forward to the next few minutes. I thought I was going to be in trouble.

I edged out on the window ledge, pulling up the chair until it lay across the gap presented by the window. I didn't need to be an engineer to work out that it should be dead centre. A little uneven pressure and the chair would come flying out of the window.

I lowered myself, carefully, pulling hard on the sheets. The chair held firm.

I put the whole of my weight on it and went down as we'd been instructed at school, using the feet and hands. I was doing very well too until a high pitched scream tore through the air and put such terror in my heart that I jerked quite involuntarily and the chair shifted in position.

I thought I'd dislodged it. I forgot about being careful. I forgot about my hands. I forgot about everything but the fact that I was dangling in space and Chrissie was somewhere below me, unprotected and vulnerable.

I shot down the rope and about four feet from the ground there was a crack, a splintering of glass and I was free flying.

It wasn't for very long. I landed with a thud that knocked every breath of air from my body and I thought I'd broken my back. The sky came down to meet me and then I felt cold water on my face.

I opened my eyes. Chrissie was bending over me, slopping water on my forehead from the same pail I had used earlier. Her breath was coming in painful little gasps.

I tried to sit up and couldn't make it. She pulled on my arm. "Oh, Nell. Oh Nell!"

"What was that noise?"

"I don't know."

"Help me up." She put every muscle to work but I was the one beaded with sweat as I stood swaying on my feet.

"Are you all right?" she said anxiously.

"Yes. Give me a minute." I breathed hard. I didn't think anything was broken, it just felt as if it was.

"Can you walk?"

"Yes." Yes, I could, crunching in broken glass, feeling as if I were broken in the same way inside and held together only by the outer skin—and that was missing too in parts, especially on my hands. They felt as if they were on fire.

I'd fainted. For how long? Long enough for Chrissie to get the bucket of water to revive me. Why hadn't Ken come out to investigate? He must have heard the glass breaking if nothing else. But the scream . . . The glass was a dropping of a pin compared with that.

"What time is it?" I peered at my watch but

the tiny face blurred and dissolved before my eyes and I held it out to Chrissie.

"Nearly eight o'clock," she said.

"Was I out for long?"

"Oh, ages," she said and some of the despair she must have felt was in her voice. "I didn't know what to do."

"Did . . . er . . . was there another scream?"

"No. It's been as quiet as anything."

I took a few tottering steps to the wall and slumped against it, trying to think.

That scream had been horrifying and I thought it had come from within the house. Ken or his visitor? Man or woman? Impossible to say. The sound had been sexless, a screeching scream that could have come from an animal. I fastened on that thought. "It could have been an owl," I told Chrissie.

"Yes." She had as much belief in that as I did but she wasn't going to argue or point out that it would be the first time an owl had strayed this way.

"We'll be on our way."

"Yes," she said again and her hand crept into mine.

"I've left a case in the garage."

Chrissie didn't release my hand for a moment.

I got the case and my bag and we walked round the side of the garage and saw the front door standing wide open, a shaft of light spilling out on to the gravelled path.

"Quietly now." I didn't need to tell Chrissie. She was already walking on tip toe.

I looked back as we were half-way down the path and somehow managed not to break my stride. The door to the den was also open and Mrs. Singer was standing with her back to me looking down on Ken. From the way he was sprawled I didn't think he would be getting up again, not ever.

So his visitor was Mrs. Singer. Somehow I'd thought . . . But he would probably assume that I would be afraid to see Mrs. Singer again after the fight we'd had.

I marched Chrissie down the road, no longer afraid of pursuit from Ken but anxious to get as far away as possible.

I didn't blame Mrs. Singer for what she'd done. I suppose I was partly to blame myself. I'd forced her to think and she must have come to the logical conclusion and gone to face Ken with it.

217

He'd said he had something on her, that she would be afraid to speak out against him, but having no feeling for his own daughter how could he guess at how Mrs. Singer felt? She had loved Betty and there is no one more frightening than a bereaved mother under the force of avenging fury, as I well knew.

The train into Manchester was due when we got to the station and we didn't have to wait for very long.

The main hotels in the city were far beyond the means of my slender purse. We took a bus ride out and booked into a small hotel where we immediately went to bed, both of us.

I was asleep within minutes and no thought of Ken disturbed my dreams. I don't think I stirred all night and it took time for Chrissie to waken me.

I had stiffened up and had to force myself to move. "I'm going for a bath," I told Chrissie. "You order what breakfast you want and have it sent up here. I'll have a pot of coffee—I don't want anything else. Oh and ask for a couple of morning papers."

She was quite happy at doing that. It made her feel grown up.

I went along to the bathroom and made the

bath as hot as I could stand it. It made me more mobile and I got dressed with a minimum of gritted teeth and involuntary grunts and groans. I was covered in bruises. The one where Ken had kicked me was the worst but I looked respectable enough when I was clothed and had make-up on. The scratches showed, but not badly, and the bruise on my chin was disguised completely. I couldn't do anything with my hands though. They were a mess.

A maid brought the tray up. I drank my coffee and read the papers while Chrissie enjoyed her breakfast. There was no mention of Ken being found and the second day's coverage of Betty's murder was relegated to the middle pages. I learned nothing new.

While Chrissie was having her bath I called the police. Egan wasn't there so I left a message telling him where we were—I wasn't going to have him think I was running away from him —and then I phoned Lee.

He wasn't in either but he'd evidently left instructions in the event of my phoning. The woman who answered said, "Would that be Miss Howard?"

I agreed it was with some caution. One of these people here at the Hall wanted me dead.

"Miss Howard—*Miss Madeleine* that is, would like to speak to you. Would you hold the line please?"

I only had to wait a couple of minutes. Madeleine's warm huskiness held a breathlessness as if she'd run.

"Lee asked me to speak to you if you called," she said. "He's phoning in every hour in the hope that you would. He wants to see you— any time and place you care to name. He said he wouldn't tell anyone but he thinks you ought to inform the police of your whereabouts. He said it could be an . . . an unwise move."

From the way she hesitated I thought she was being polite, editing his actual words and a small flame flared. Who was he to tell me what to do? "I've already informed the police," I said coldly. "I wasn't running away from them."

"Oh, I'm sure he didn't mean to imply . . ." Her voice trailed off. She knew damn well that was exactly what he'd meant. He'd told her all about me, probably in detail. I wondered just what was between those two and wondering that didn't make that small flame burn any lower. She changed the subject abruptly. "Have you phoned your father?"

"No."

"I think you ought to. He's worried about you. Lee saw your stepfather yesterday afternoon."

"And now he believes there might be something in what I say? Amazing what a difference personal appraisal makes! I don't give him many points for perception though. Ken's veneer was slipping yesterday. He usually puts on a much better show."

"You—You know about Lee's visit?"

"Yes." And then because I didn't want to explain I said, "I'm with Chrissie now." I gave her the name of the hotel and the phone number and asked her to tell only Lee.

"Not even your father? He wants you here, Elinor. This is your home now."

"Are all your family of the same opinion?" I asked drily.

She hesitated. "Well, it's been rather a shock. My mother—"

"She knew about me. She probably helped to get rid of us. All these years she's kept silent."

"I'd like to defend her," Madeleine said in a low voice, "but right at this moment I can't. It was unforgivable. She'll find excuses, see no wrong in it herself. You see I know her. I've got no illusions left. She'll try to give you a hard time but your father has warned her. If she upsets you she'll have to leave the Hall. Phone your father, Elinor. You've got the number, haven't you?"

"Yes—but I can't phone him. Not yet."

"Why not?"

"Maybe because I don't want to bring any more trouble on him; maybe because I've got too much pride. I don't know, Madeleine. I'm going to need some money. I was going to ask Lee to arrange it for me. I don't think I could find the words to ask my father myself."

"How much do you need?"

"Enough to keep us for a little while. This hotel isn't one of the expensive ones but it's not cheap either. I was going to ask for fifty pounds."

"I can let you have that. Right away."

"No. I can't take it from you. I—"

There was a knock on the door. I thought it was Chrissie. "Hold on a moment."

It was Egan and Turpin.

I blinked at them. "Goodness! That was quick. Excuse me a moment." I went back to the phone. "I'll have to go, Madeleine. The police are here."

"But—"

"Just tell Lee, will you?" I replaced the receiver over her protests and turned to Egan. They had shut the door and entered the room. Their faces were grave and Turpin made no attempt to get out his notebook.

"We'd like you to come down to the station with us," Egan said.

"All right," I said agreeably. "Chrissie is having a bath. I'll go and hurry her up."

"No. You stay here."

I regarded him in surprise. "You don't imagine I'll try to get away, do you? After telling you where I was?"

"Telling us?"

"I phoned about ten minutes ago. I daresay I should have done it last night but I was too tired."

"We've been looking all night for you," Egan said explosively.

"Well, I'm sorry. But how was I to know?"

"You know your stepfather's dead?"

"No!" I said flatly.

"You don't seem very surprised."

"What would you like me to do? Faint at the news? You know what I thought of him."

"You wanted him dead, didn't you?"

"Dead or behind bars. It didn't really matter.

He was everything I said. He admitted killing Betty."

"When?"

"Yesterday afternoon. He told me that someone had offered him two hundred pounds to put me out of the way for a while. To avert a scandal he said. Then when he found out my father was alive and that I was his legitimate daughter he realized he'd been had. I imagine he got quite nasty about that but he got a better offer. Five thousand pounds to arrange an 'accident' for me."

"Why should he tell you this?"

"Because Ken was a blackmailer. Five thousand wasn't enough for him. He thought he'd discovered an income for life and he had plans for us—like foisting us all on my father and living at Winters Hall. He thought he could get me to go along with this. He offered protection from this . . . person who wanted me dead."

"Didn't he tell you who it was?"

"Oh no! He had to keep that up his sleeve. It's someone at the Hall. He was anticipating great pleasure in living on top of them, constantly turning the screw."

Egan looked at Turpin. They exchanged a long stare of silent communication that excluded me, then Egan said, "You'd better get your coat."

"Don't you believe me?"

"Your coat."

I was putting it on when Chrissie returned and I said quickly, "These men are from the police, Chrissie. They want me to answer some questions. There's nothing to worry about. You can come along—" I shot a look at Egan. "She can come, can't she? I don't want to leave her here on her own."

He nodded.

"All right then. Let's get you dressed."

She looked in askance at the two men and I said hurriedly, "If you'd just turn your backs."

"We'll wait downstairs for you, Miss Howard," Egan said.

So they no longer thought I'd run away. I suppose that was a good sign.

We got downstairs over ten minutes later and I left the key at the desk. The clerk there eyed me with a kind of uneasy curiosity. He was probably wondering what category of criminal to slot us in. I hoped I wouldn't be confronted with the bill and the news that the room was no longer available when we returned. For one thing I didn't think I'd have enough money to pay.

The car wasn't noticeably a police car but the first thing Egan did was to call in and check whether I had left the address of the hotel for him.

Chrissie said, "Is it about my father?"

She had to be told sometime and I didn't think it would upset her. I said matter of factly, "He's dead, Chrissie. Someone killed him."

"Was that him screaming then?"

"It could have been."

"What was that?" Egan demanded.

"We heard a scream."

"And you didn't try to find out who had made it?" He sounded both incredulous and disbelieving.

"I'm no heroine," I said bluntly. "All I wanted was to get away. Ken had locked us in Chrissie's room. You must have seen the sheets we tied together. I'd lowered Chrissie down and was hanging in mid air when that scream came. It frightened me so much it dislodged me. When I was compos mentis again I wasn't going looking for more trouble."

"What time did this happen?" he said quickly.

"All I can tell you is what time it was when it was all over. It was nearly eight o'clock, wasn't it, Chrissie?"

"Just after ten minutes to," she confirmed. "I looked at Nell's watch. She couldn't see."

"And we got the eight thirty train into Manchester," I added.

"We know that," Egan said absently. "Are you saying you lost consciousness for a time?"

"Yes."

"For how long? Estimate it."

"I haven't the vaguest idea."

"It was a long time," Chrissie said, remembrance giving a quiver to her voice. "A very long time."

"Half an hour?"

"Oh. I don't know. I shook her and then I waited. And then I thought some water . . . I filled the bucket and wet my handkerchief and kept putting it on her face."

"You heard nothing from the house?"

"No."

"How did you find out about it, Inspector?" I said.

"We had a call from your neighbour, Mr. Jennings. Apparently he was taking his dog out around ten o'clock when he saw a man trying

227

to get in the house. A prudent man, Mr. Jennings. He phoned the police before investigating and when he came out again the man had gone. He took the number of the car that had been outside though. We managed to trace it to a car hire firm. It wasn't until this morning that we were able to find out who had rented it however. We picked him up about an hour ago. Your friend, Mr. Dexter. He refuses to talk to us. And do you know why, Miss Howard? I believe he thinks you killed your stepfather."

9

"HE can't think that," I said, feeling cold all over.

"Perhaps you'll be able to convince him of it." Egan said no more. His tone wasn't exactly hopeful.

I stared out of the window. The car was travelling swiftly. We were already out of Manchester. How could Lee think I had killed Ken? But of course he didn't know me. As I didn't know him. Why had he been trying to break in? Was he so concerned about me? Did he think Ken was refusing to answer the door because he knew who was outside?

I was glad when we reached the police station. At least it put a stop to my thoughts— but I didn't see a sign of Lee.

I was taken into a little room where I repeated everything I had already told Egan and answered more of his questions. He wasn't unfriendly, merely impersonal and very polite.

It was fortunate I didn't have to lie. The omission of seeing Mrs. Singer was easy to maintain. He never asked if I'd looked back. But then he didn't know the door had been open and it was possible for anyone to see into the den.

He went over and over what Ken had said to me that afternoon. I couldn't remember it word for word. He tripped me up a couple of times but it wasn't on anything that mattered. At least I didn't think so. Then he switched tactics and I had to go over the afternoon of Betty's death again.

I had coffee, several cups. I needed it. My throat kept drying up and then when I was asked to describe the scene when Mrs. Singer had attacked me I found myself stuttering.

I didn't want to talk about Mrs. Singer. I didn't want her to be caught. Ken deserved everything he got.

It must have been nearly lunchtime when my statement was typed and brought to me to sign and then I was left alone for a while.

Egan returned about half an hour later. He was without his shadow. "We gave Mr. Dexter your statement to read," he said, "and he very kindly agreed to make a statement himself. Your stepfather had told him you'd run away because you were afraid of being arrested. He'd

230

believed it at first. He thought you might have gone to your father. He went back to the Hall but you didn't turn up or phone and he got to thinking about it and realized you would never have left your half-sister for long. He went back because he thought your stepfather could have been lying and was keeping you out of his way. He broke in because he thought you might be locked in your room. He found your stepfather and he drew his own conclusions from the broken window and the fallen sheets.

His tone was lightly sardonic—as if Lee had been very foolish.

I said, "You came to the same conclusion yourself with far more facts to go on."

"Not so, Miss Howard. We merely wanted you to make a statement. We didn't come to arrest you. Are you going back to the hotel?"

"Yes."

"Perhaps it's just as well. We've not finished with the house yet. I'd send you in a car but I think Mr. Dexter will want to take you. He won't be very long now."

"Have you found out any more about Ken?" I was sorry I'd tried to defend Lee. He saw too much.

"No. It will be easier now perhaps." He went

over to the window and stood playing with the cord from the blinds, absently staring at the street outside. He murmured, "You did know he was dead, didn't you?"

"I thought it was an almost certain probability," I said carefully. "He didn't come after us, you see."

"Yes." He swung round and I felt his eyes boring into me, no longer absent, but hard and knowing. "You're keeping something back but your sister bears you out in every detail. She's not lying. She couldn't."

"I'm not lying either," I said with dignity.

"Do you believe this . . . this person who was willing to pay five thousand pounds for your death is the one who killed your stepfather?"

I didn't care if the blame for Ken's death went there. I said, "From what Ken said before he went downstairs I assumed he was expecting him. What do *you* imagine his reaction would be when he was told what Ken had in mind for his future? I don't imagine anyone would take kindly to the idea of being blackmailed for life."

"You think it's a man?"

"I don't know. I've not really thought about it."

"I believe your cousin Patrick was under the impression he would be the next heir."

"Did Lee tell you that? Yes . . . I suppose he did. I've upset his applecart by turning up out of the blue. Maybe you could find out where he was last night."

"We'll do that," he said blandly, "and more besides. Ah, here's Mr. Dexter."

Lee stood in the doorway, his eyes wary and hostile.

Egan coughed. "I asked Miss Howard to wait. I thought you'd want the privilege of seeing her back to the hotel."

"You've brought my car here?"

"Yes. It's outside. A word of warning before you leave, Mr. Dexter. Miss Howard's life may be in danger. Don't try to conceal any more facts from us. You could be making a mistake." He walked towards the door, holding Lee's gaze, and very softly he added, "We're not stupid men, Mr. Dexter. Bear that in mind."

Lee didn't answer. He stood aside to let Egan pass and looked at me.

"Why didn't you get in touch with me?" he said harshly.

"I couldn't very well. It was difficult."

"Difficult!"

"I phoned this morning. I spoke to Madeleine." An antagonism was between us, suspicion and bitterness on both sides. "I got your message to give myself up. I'm surprised you managed to keep silent when the police got hold of you."

"Do you imagine—" He cut the words off. "You little fool," he said shortly. "Come on. You're going home to your father."

"No. Not to Winters Hall."

"Why not?"

"Because someone there wants me dead," I said flaring up. "Didn't you read that statement properly or do you think it's another instance of my over-imaginative mind? You didn't believe me about Ken, did you? You thought I was making it all up. What reason did you figure out for my doing that? I'd like to know. Tell me. Just a silly hysterical female or did I have something more devious in mind? Was I perhaps preparing the ground for a murderous attack on Ken?"

He crossed the floor angrily and for a moment stood staring at me speechlessly and then he suddenly grabbed me and his mouth was on mine, hard and certain, and there was no more anger between us.

Someone cleared their throat in a kind of apologetic fashion. Lee drew back and glanced behind him. Egan was in the doorway. "Excuse me," he said expressionlessly and he looked at me. "Your sister is waiting in the car for you."

"Thank you."

I walked unsteadily towards the door, aware my cheeks were a flaming red.

Lee followed me. "Don't leave the hotel without letting us know where you're going, Miss Howard." Egan said.

"No."

"And don't do anything foolish."

I thought he was referring to the scene he had just witnessed. I snapped at him, "I'm not in the habit of behaving foolishly—over anything."

He nodded fractionally and turned away.

The yellow Capri was at the kerb outside. Chrissie was in the back, perched on the edge of the seat, her gaze strained towards the entrance to the police station.

Her smile lit up her face as I came out and she relaxed visibly but as she saw Lee behind me she sank back in some confusion.

I shared her feeling. I felt confused myself. I looked at Lee and couldn't believe that only minutes before he'd kissed me. He was grim and remote.

"Where is this hotel?" he asked.

I told him and gave him directions. I'd gone in the back with Chrissie and I remained silent for most of the journey, listening with only half an ear as Chrissie told me she'd seen all round the police station and had been given milk and buttered teacakes by a policewoman.

Lee drove into the car park of the hotel. It was only small, with room for about a dozen cars. He switched off the engine and said abruptly, "I still think you should go home. It's what your father wants."

"Would you guarantee my safety?"

"I can't believe that—" He broke off, his gaze going past me. "I'll see you to your room," he said.

"What is it? What have you seen?" I turned around but I couldn't see anything out of the ordinary.

Lee didn't answer. He got out of the car and started walking to the hotel entrance.

Chrissie said, "What did Lee mean? *Your* father?"

I looked down at her. Of course Chrissie didn't know. Now how did I explain that?

"He's not dead after all," I said. "He lives at Winters Hall."

"And are we going to live with him now my father is dead?"

"I don't know." Reduced into the simplest terms. I suppose it seemed logical enough to Chrissie.

"Is he nice?" she asked. "A real father like Mr. Jennings?"

"Well, I don't know, Chrissie. I think he's very nice but he was in an accident during the war and it's spoilt his face. He doesn't like people seeing him because they might be frightened."

"I wouldn't be frightened."

"No, of course not." We went through the hotel doors and I realized why Lee had gone before us. He'd seen a car he recognized. Madeleine's. She was sitting on the couch that Egan and Turpin had occupied earlier.

She got up as we approached, brushing aside the question Lee had hurled at her with a smile.

"I had to come," she said simply. "I didn't know you'd be here. You didn't phone on the hour as you said you would."

"I couldn't," he said. "I was with the police."

"Your stepfather's dead, isn't he?" she said looking directly at me. "You used the past tense. I noticed it right away. I thought it better not to comment at the time but I told your father and he made some enquiries. He insists that you come home. I've paid your bill here and I got the maid to pack your case. You can't stay here, Elinor. Forget your pride. There's Chrissie to consider too." She smiled at Chrissie. "You'd like to come home with me, wouldn't you? You liked the Hall."

"Oh yes," Chrissie breathed.

"That's settled then."

"Wait a minute . . ." I protested.

"No," Lee said. "She's right. This is no place for you. We can look after you at the Hall. You go with Madeleine, Chrissie. I'll bring your sister." He picked up the case Madeleine had stowed by the side of the couch.

I looked from one to the other. Short of making a scene I didn't see what I could do. And why fight it? I would have to face up to it sometime. I wasn't in a position to be independent.

I followed Lee. He wasn't giving me much chance to make a scene. He was already out of the hotel. He put the case in the boot and waited for me to get in the car and we were off on another silent journey, Madeleine's car just ahead of us. She had a little sports car and she drove it well.

I sank down in the seat and put my head against the back of it, closing my eyes.

I was suddenly deathly tired. I didn't want to bother anymore—about anything. I had kept calm, I had acted in a way I thought best. I had answered all those questions, I had been kissed by Lee, by a stranger whose mind was closed to mine. Why had he done it? He had been angry with me. He still was. And I didn't really know the reason for that either.

"When did you eat last?"

"W-what?" The question jolted me out of my self-absorption.

"You look like death."

"I'm not hungry." And I wasn't. I'd long gone past that stage. The thought of food made me feel sick.

"I think we'll stop for some lunch." He shot past Madeleine, gesticulated and turned into one of the Little Chef places that were so conveniently dotted along the roads.

Madeleine slid into place at the side of us and got out.

"We're going to eat," Lee said.

"A good idea. They'll be tied up at home with the visitors."

He didn't ask what I wanted. A bowl of soup was placed before me and then a steak with a green salad.

I ate. Once I started I couldn't stop. I felt it had been a week since I'd last eaten.

Madeleine had won Chrissie's heart. She had a way with children but then I'd noticed that before. She had a way with Lee too. I wasn't so intent on my food to fail to notice the kind of instinctive understanding that existed between them.

Back in the car I said abruptly, "Are you going to marry Madeleine?"

He didn't look at me. "Why do you ask?"

"You seem to be on very good terms with her."

"And so I am."

Subject closed. I didn't say another word. I had been put in my place. A solitary kiss didn't give me the right to ask any questions.

"We'll go up to your father right away," Lee said as he turned in the drive leading to the Hall.

"Chrissie too?"

"Yes. Madeleine will be busy."

I'd forgotten it was Saturday. The gardens were dotted with people.

Lee went round the back of the house and drove carefully through an arched entrance, swinging the car around over cobbled stones to one of a row of garages which made up one side of the square.

Madeleine swung in beside him. Five spaces for five cars. They must have had a great many horses at one time. One side remained untouched, the upper halves of two of the stalls were open and I half expected a horse to poke his head through to see what the noise was.

Chrissie scrambled out. "Do you have horses?" she said in awe.

"A couple," Madeleine said with a smile. "We'll have to see about getting you a pony later on. Would you like that?"

"Oh *yes*."

Madeleine ruffled her silken head lightly. "I'll have to go now. Remember what I told you."

"What did she tell you?" I asked in a low voice as she went up to Lee and spoke softly to him.

"She was telling me about your father—how

brave he was and that he was a very kind man. Do you remember the story of Beauty and the Beast, Nell?"

"Yes."

"She told it to me again."

I looked across at Madeleine. Her face was grave as she talked to Lee and then she smiled as he said something. She was beautiful. I wanted to dislike her but I couldn't. She had sympathy and understanding and the special kind of rapport that made her someone out of the ordinary.

Chrissie turned abruptly at the sound of a horse's hooves striking the cobbles.

Madeleine left Lee's side and came quickly over to us. It was almost as if she were giving us her protection.

"My brother Patrick, I think," she murmured.

He came out of the shadows of the low arch like a young God, tall and straight in the saddle, the sun striking on his hair and giving him a helmet of dark ebony.

A pretty boy, the vicar had said. But he was more than that. I had seen him before in the great paintings, in the statues of the ancient Greeks. There was the same purity, the classic features, the perfect symmetry of bone and muscle.

He reined in, surveying us all coolly and then he slid down from the saddle in a fluid, easy movement that held as much grace as the mocking courtier's bow he performed before me. "Cousin Elinor, I presume?"

A small sigh escaped Madeleine. It sounded like relief. "Yes," she said. "And this is Chrissie. They're going up to see Uncle Terence now."

"Then don't let me stop you." He smiled at me and then at Chrissie who was staring open-mouthed at him. I wondered if she'd changed her mind about marrying Lee. Patrick was a far more glamorous figure. But his smile, charming though it was, didn't extend to his eyes. They were brilliant eyes, as blue as an Alpine gentian, but the brilliance was cold and more than a little chilling. I recognized the voice too. He'd been the one who had put the phone down on me at the Hall. Not that I could condemn him for that, if as Lee said, it was normal practice to deny my father's existence.

"Come along," Lee said, almost as if we were both children who needed to be hustled on their way.

We went in through the kitchen, an airy, spacious room dominated by an Aga backed up with a lot of Hygena fittings. A woman preparing some half-dozen salad bowls smiled at us and uttered a cheerful greeting to Lee.

He made a rejoinder but didn't pause in his stride, going straight across the stone flagged floor to the stairs.

My father was in his chair, hidden again from view.

Lee said evenly, "I've brought them—both of them."

I was afraid of Chrissie's reaction. She stood frozen at my side as my father got slowly to his feet.

"Hello, father," I said unsteadily.

He smiled but it was uncertain and wavering and his eyes flicked to Chrissie. Her breath was expelled in a long sigh. "I'm Chrissie," she said. "I'm very pleased to meet you," and she stepped forward like a little lady, extending her hand.

My father hesitated and then took it gravely, "How do you do?"

"My father's dead," Chrissie announced. "Are we really going to live here now?"

"If you would like that."

"Oh yes, I think so. My father wasn't a very nice man, you know. I'm glad he's dead." She smiled at him without the slightest affectation. "I think I'm going to like you."

His eyes went over her small flower-like face feature by feature, searching, perhaps remembering. He said to me, "You were right. She is like her mother."

"Yes." I met his eyes steadily. "She did believe you were dead. She would never have left you."

"I know. I made Beryl tell the truth." He sat down as though weary. "I can't blame my mother entirely. I should have had more faith; I should have known she could never—But that's all past. It's the future we have to look to now. Lee—perhaps you'd take Chrissie down to the kitchen and superintend some tea for us?"

"Right." I think he'd been expecting the command. My father waved me to a chair. "So your stepfather is dead. Do you know who did it?"

"Why do you ask that?" I said slowly. "Have you been talking to Egan?"

"I had a few words with him. He'll be coming out here."

"Oh! I never phoned him. He said I had to let him know if I moved out of the hotel." I jumped to my feet but he waved me down again.

"It's all right. I told him you were coming here."

"You were so sure I'd come?"

"This is your home," he said evenly. "I don't want you ever to forget that. Now tell me everything you know, everything that has happened to you."

It wasn't like telling Egan. My father listened in complete silence and when I'd finished he said, "Did you believe your stepfather when he said he'd been offered so much money?"

"He lied when it suited him but there was no reason for it this time. And he was angry that he'd been duped."

"Do you think he made the initial contact?"

"I don't know. He was quick at picking things up but he assumed like Betty that I was illegitimate. It was logical to him that I should be discredited and one thing followed another. He'd not planned to kill Betty but when she threatened to bring him into it it was inevitable what he'd do next. And then he found out you were still alive and the possibilities were enormous."

"Beryl kept quiet all these years. She knew about you. She would have guessed who you were the minute she heard what happened that Saturday afternoon. She would be the natural person for your stepfather to see if he came here." My father stared down at his hands. "She would be afraid of my finding out about you. Her first thought would be to keep you away at all costs. She wouldn't think of killing you, not at first, but I don't think she would hesitate if she thought it the only solution." He raised his head. "Patrick is her one love. She would go to any lengths to protect what she considered was his."

"What about Patrick himself?"

"Yes. I can't overlook that possibility but I can't see him offering anyone five thousand pounds. He would do the job himself."

"It was Mrs. Singer who killed Ken," I said abruptly. "I saw her."

He stiffened, his eyes searching my face. "You feel she's done you a favour?"

"No, no. It's not that. But I think she had justification. No one should be sent to prison for exterminating vermin."

"You should have told the police."

"Perhaps. But I'm not going to and you're not going to say anything, are you? You can't."

"What did you see?"

"It was when we were going down the path. I looked back. The front door was open and I could see into the den. She was standing over his body."

"Did she see you?"

"I don't think she would have noticed if the fire engines were going off at full blast."

"Egan knows you're holding back something."

"Yes, I know. He warned me."

"He thinks you might be in danger."

"Do you?"

"I don't know. This changes things. But we'll find out the truth." His mouth was set grimly. "If you go anywhere Madeleine or Lee will go with you."

"Do you really think it was your sister-in-law who offered that money?"

"Yes, I'm afraid so. For one thing she's the only one with ready access to such a large amount. Patrick and Madeleine have most of their money tied up in trust funds."

"Have you talked to her?"

"Not about that. I've not had the opportunity since I spoke to Egan, but I will certainly do so before the police give her warning."

"And what will you do if she admits it?"

"She will leave this house. That's the worst thing that I could do to her. In fact, I'm seriously considering doing that in any case. I don't think it was entirely my mother's idea to get rid of you and your mother. Beryl would have been thinking of Patrick even then."

"Did we live here? In this room I mean?"

"Yes! Banished in her own home. Neither of them would have liked me to find out about that either. They must have panicked when that telegram arrived telling them I was still alive." His tone was very bitter. "I never believed in the curse. Everyone has bad luck at one time or another—but this family has had more than its fair share. When I'm gone you might be wise to leave the Hall. You'll have a fair income."

"Right now I'm more concerned with my luck at present, not years ahead in the future." I smiled at him. "I've not quite taken all that in yet. You'll look after Chrissie, won't you?"

"Of course. She's a nice child." He rested his head against the back of his chair. "I think they're coming back now. I've had rooms prepared for you. Lee will show you where they are when we've had tea. They are in the private wing we don't show. It was the nursery at one time and I think Chrissie will like it."

She more than liked it. She was absolutely enthralled. There were plenty of signs of past generations of Howard children. Books and toys and dolls, an old rocking horse, a cupboard full of objects that fascinated me as much as Chrissie.

My room led off it, a smaller room than Chrissie's but even then larger than my own bedroom at home. Home! That had never been my home. I had a feeling I was going to feel differently now.

"Like it?" Lee asked.

"It's lovely." I went to the small casement window. It looked out over the sunken lawn where we'd had tea. It seemed a century ago since then. There was a bowl of flowers on the deep ledge. Madeleine's doing I suspected.

I turned around. Lee's head almost touched the low ceiling. It was simply furnished; dark rosewood furniture, a single bed, plain white walls, flowered curtains.

"Once you've been in it a week or so it will look different again," he commented. "It's bare now, unstamped by any personality—but even so it's better than any hotel room. I'll get your case."

I would have to get more clothes. I wondered if he'd mind taking me over the next day—after I'd cleared it with Egan. Chrissie was all right for a week or more but I'd not brought much for myself.

I asked him when he got back and he didn't think there would be any difficulty about it. "Did your father warn you about not leaving this house on your own?"

"Yes."

"See that you don't forget."

I flushed. "I'm not a child you know and I have a highly developed sense of self-preservation."

"One wouldn't imagine so to look at you. I suppose you did that damage to your hands on the sheets. Didn't it occur to you what friction can do?"

"When a scream goes off in your ears you don't worry about a small amount of skin, you take the whole of it into consideration and you get out of the way as fast as you can." There it was again. That strange antagonism. I said abruptly, "What are you holding back from the police?"

"What am *I*? You say that as if you're guilty of it too."

"Too. Exactly! And I asked you first."

"Well, I did wipe the handle of the knife."

The knife! It was a knife again. I'd not asked Egan. It had never even occurred to me to ask how Ken had been killed. But of course Mrs. Singer would use the same method. She would think of it as just retribution. "I thought it best not to confess to that," Lee said easily. "I expect I was only adding an extra polish in any event. People think of things like that these days."

"Except you were afraid I might not have had the wit to do it."

"You could have panicked. He didn't die right away. A messy job—and a bloody one. I don't think the murderer would have got away without the signs of the crime on his clothing —or her clothing—as the case maybe."

"Oh!" Mrs. Singer's coat had been black. I wondered if she'd noticed. It probably wouldn't show up but if the police suspected her a laboratory examination would reveal it at once.

I was suddenly aware of Lee's narrowed gaze

on me. He surely didn't still suspect me. Did he think I could have made all that up and even got Chrissie to lie for me? "Why do you look at me like that?" I demanded.

"If you don't know it doesn't matter. I'll see you at dinner."

"Wait a minute."

He paused in the act of ducking his head to get through the narrow low doorway.

"How long are you staying here? Don't you have a job to get back to?"

His eyebrows went up. "Throwing your weight around already? I'd settle in first." He shut the door quietly behind him, thwarting my instant desire to hurl something at his head.

I took a deep breath, told myself to calm down and unpacked the case, taking Chrissie's things into her room. She was trying the rocking horse for size.

I found a bathroom next door. I didn't go exploring further. After that remark of Lee's I was going to be careful. No one was going to accuse me of thrusting myself forward.

Madeleine paid us a visit about six o'clock. She knocked on my door and then came through into the nursery room as I called out.

"Dinner's at seven," she said. "I'll take you down. Everything all right?"

"Yes, fine. I wonder though if I could use the phone."

"Sure. We'll have to get an extension put in here. The nearest one is in my bedroom."

She had one of the rooms that were put on view but with the disappearance of the guide rope and the roll of carpet it looked different. Or maybe it was because I now knew Madeleine and could recognize the way in which she had made it her own.

I wondered if that was what Lee meant. This room was certainly stamped with Madeleine's personality; elegant, beautiful, very feminine. He'd have seen it of course.

"I'll leave you to it," Madeleine said. "You can find your own way back, can't you?"

I nodded. The phone was by the bed but there was no directory handy. I called after her but she'd gone.

The directory was probably in the library. I made my way downstairs. It was astonishing how different the house was now. I met no one and found the directory on one of the library shelves.

I looked up Mrs. Singer's number and dialled

it. She answered on the tenth ring when I was just about to replace the receiver.

Her voice was cracked and there was more than a little apprehension in it.

"This is Elinor Howard," I said in a low voice. "Don't be alarmed by what I say. I just want to warn you. If you've not got rid of that black coat of yours do it now, at once. There could be blood on it."

I put the receiver down without waiting for a reply and replaced the directory, then I turned to the door and froze in shock.

Lee was standing there. I knew he'd heard every word. He stared at me with quite the blankest face I've ever seen.

"An accomplice!" he said. "I *thought* I'd worried you with that remark about the blood."

10

IT was a few seconds before I could find my voice. How could he? How *could* he?

"Don't be perfectly ridiculous," I snapped.

"How else can you explain those words?"

"I don't have to explain to you. Not a thing."

"If you don't I'll be the next person using that phone and it will be to the police."

"You wouldn't!" I stared at him and felt more than saw the implacable intent. He would. Without any hesitation. There could never be any justification for murder in his eyes.

"I give you my word that I had nothing to do with my stepfather's death," I said stiffly.

"But you do know who did it, don't you? Don't you understand that withholding such information makes you an accessory to the crime?"

"I don't care. He murdered Betty. He deserved to die. He'd have wriggled out of anything the police tried to pin on him and gone right on doing evil. I can't blame her for what she did and I'm not going to say a word to the police. You can phone them. I'll not stop you. But I'll deny anything you say."

"It's the mother, isn't it? The girl's mother."

"I'm not telling you anything."

"You little fool! Don't you understand what you're doing? You've done more than warn her. You've told her that you know what she's done. What do you think she's going to do now? What would be the normal reaction?"

"You mean that she's likely to turn her attention to me? Try to kill me next? To shut my mouth?" I raised my eyebrows scornfully. "And that's about as ridiculous as assuming I had anything to do with the murder. Would I have warned her if I was going to tell anyone?"

"Some people don't think logically. She'll only know she's not as safe as she thought she was."

"She won't try to murder me."

"Didn't she try once?"

"That was when she thought I'd killed Betty," I said slowly.

He shook his head at me. "It's not good enough. If you don't phone the police I will."

"And what will you tell them? I'll deny this conversation ever took place."

"You're not a good liar, Elinor. I think Egan will get what he needs from you."

"Why should you interfere?" I cried, knowing too well that all Egan would need was a hint. "What do you care about it all? It's nothing to do with you—not in any respect."

"I'll tell you why I care," he said coldly. "I don't want to see you stretched out on a mortuary slab somewhere. I'm going to see your father now. You can let me know at dinner what you've decided to do."

"I am *not* telling the police anything about Mrs. Singer."

"Think about it," he said impassively. "You've got a lot to lose."

I watched him go and then turned back to look at the phone. But it was no use. I couldn't ring the police. It was worse than being a Judas.

I dialled Mrs. Singer's number again. It rang out, on and on. I could picture her looking at the phone, afraid to pick it up. Somehow I knew she was there but I had to recognize failure. She wasn't going to answer.

I went back upstairs to join Chrissie but she wasn't alone. Beryl Howard was with her, clutching a doll to her meagre bosom as if it were a child. "Don't let me catch you touching any of these things," she was saying. "You've no right to them. "You're nothing but a—"

"Good evening, Mrs. Howard," I said coldly and I went over to Chrissie. She was looking bewildered and more than a little upset. I put my arms on her shoulders and stood facing Beryl. "If the doll belongs to you, Mrs. Howard, I suggest you keep it in your own room. Chrissie has every right to play with whatever she chooses in this room. My father has given her that right. You needn't imagine that you can treat us as you treated our mother. This is our home now and you'll be the one to leave if there is any trouble. Perhaps my father didn't make that perfectly clear."

Her eyes were blazing, her face white with fury with two spots of colour burning high on her cheeks. "Who do you think you are, talking to me like that? I give the orders in this house. I've been giving them for the last twenty years and if you imagine you're going to turn me out you're very much mistaken. I got rid of you once and I'll do it again. Your *father* indeed! He's a sick man, not in his right mind. He'd have been put away years ago if I'd had any sense—and I'll do it now. I'll get him certified."

"Mother!" Madeleine's voice was like a whip-lash. Beryl cringed and then turned slowly. "I was only . . . I was only—It's so unfair," she burst out and she was in full spate once again. "Why did she have to find out about us? I arranged it all so cleverly. I put the fear of God into that wretched girl. No kitchenmaid was going to rule here at Winters Hall. She had to go—otherwise something terrible would have happened to that brat of hers. It was the curse. I told her what could happen. I told her the only way she could escape was to go and never come back. I told her she had to give up every right she had. I told her—"

Madeleine slapped her hand across her mother's face and the rush of words was cut off like a dammed waterfall, just a little trickle escaping. "No one can escape the curse—not if they stay here. I wasn't lying. I never told her one lie."

"You just *forgot* to mention my father was alive," I said bitterly.

"Alive you call it!" She was off again, almost screaming. "I meant what I said. If you don't go I'll get him certified, I can do it. I can do anything."

Madeleine grabbed her by the shoulders and

propelled her from the room as if she were a bag of bones, brutally and nastily.

"Who's she?" Chrissie whispered.

"Madeleine's mother," I answered.

"I don't like her. She frightened me. She snatched that doll out of my hands and called me a funny name."

"Forget about her. If she does anything else tell me straight away." I picked up the brush and started to tidy her hair. Anything to take the shake out of my hands. My poor mother.

"I'm sorry about that," Madeleine said, returning. "It's not really sunk in with her yet. Defeat is not something she recognizes easily. I came to take you down to dinner. Are you ready?"

I said soberly, "I don't think she could ever accept us."

"She'll accept you sooner than leave the Hall. Don't worry about her. Give her a little more time." Madeleine put her hand on my arm. "Believe me I know how you feel but I can handle her. She'll behave from now on. You'll see."

She came down for dinner. I was surprised. Even more surprised at the way she conducted herself. No one could have guessed that a little

261

while before she had been involved in a scene like that. She was charming and gracious, the perfect hostess, and if she did make it obvious that Chrissie and I were to be regarded as no more than temporary visitors I wouldn't have minded that so much if I hadn't known what must have been in her thoughts the whole time. A cold calculating woman who had played on the mind of a woman without guile or subterfuge, a woman filled with the superstitions of the countryside, who had run sooner than let her child be touched by an ancient curse.

Madeleine watched her the whole time making no effort to conceal what she was doing, pointedly cutting across her words if at any time she considered it was something we could take exception to. She was backed up by her brother who would smoothly direct the flow of conversation along a different line.

I wondered if Lee noticed. He had arrived late and he spoke very little during the meal, asking me as we went in the drawing-room for coffee if I had made up my mind.

"I've not changed it if that's what you mean," I said with a snap in my voice.

"Very well."

I caught his arm. "I'll never forgive you if you tell them."

"And what does that mean?" He looked down at me, an odd expression on his face.

"Hands off," Patrick murmured in my ear. "He doesn't go with the house."

I went scarlet, dropping my hold on Lee's arm at once, and Patrick smiled at me, handing me coffee in a wafer thin china cup of miniscule proportions. "It was a joke," he said. "You were supposed to laugh."

"It wasn't exactly in the best of taste," Madeleine said tartly. "Shall I take Chrissie to bed, Elinor? She's looking rather tired."

"No, I'll take her." I swallowed my coffee. It only took two seconds. "And I think I'll have an early night myself. If you'll excuse me." I took Chrissie by the hand and she gravely said good night to everyone.

Lee ruffled her hair. "Good night, little one. Sleep well."

She smiled at him, her lovely little face upturned to his, and Mrs. Howard remarked suddenly, "It's her all over again. It's horrible! Horrible!"

"Mother!" Madeleine said warningly hurrying over to where she was sitting on the couch. "You promised. Remember, you promised."

"I can't stand to look at her."

I pulled Chrissie out of the drawing-room and made for the stairs. I couldn't face another scene.

"What did she mean?" Chrissie said in bewilderment. "What did I do?"

"You remind her of mother. You're very like her, you know. Take no notice. She won't be here very long."

"And what will you do when you're rid of her. Start on Madeleine and me next?" I missed a step. I hadn't realized Patrick had followed us out.

"You over-rate my powers of persuasion," I said over my shoulder. "My father can make his own decisions."

"Ah, but will he? Won't he be influenced by your likes and dislikes?"

"If it comes to that I like Madeleine very much indeed."

"You do? Maybe you're not aware she's going to marry Lee."

This time it was my heart that skipped. I said stiffly, "I don't see what difference that makes. As a matter of fact I had already gathered that."

"Had you?" His amazingly blue eyes were mocking. "I was under the impression you yourself were casting your eyes in that direction. Of course you might pull it off but you make a move now to get rid of us and you'll be saying good-bye to Lee as well. I just thought I'd mention it."

"I've no intention of trying to get rid of you," I said angrily.

"How strange! I'm afraid if I were in your position I'd feel rather differently. You've heard of the curse I suppose."

"Did it worry you when you thought Winters Hall was going to be yours?" I said softly.

His handsome face flushed. Patrick or his mother. Yes, I could believe it of either of them. Neither wanted me here. "You'll be sorry you came here," he said. "You'll see."

I turned my back on him. "Come on, Chrissie."

At the top of the stairs I glanced back. He was standing motionless, watching us. A shiver went down my back. I hurried Chrissie along the gallery and through into the private wing.

She was asleep almost as soon as her head touched the pillow.

I sat by her bedside for a little while and then went up to see my father.

I didn't tell him of his sister-in-law's threat, I didn't mention any of his family. We talked of books and music and I played for a little while. I left him feeling strangely comforted, the ache in my heart a little soothed.

So Madeleine was to marry Lee. Why couldn't he have told me when I'd asked?

I pushed open the pivoted panelling and found myself almost in his arms. His hand was outstretched to push it from his side. "I was looking for you," he said.

"Why?" A second later and he'd have taken a step inside. We'd have been together in the darkness with the scent of lavender all around us. I wondered what would have happened then. I stepped forward, angry with myself. Such thoughts were stupid. "I said I wouldn't leave the house alone. Can't you even trust me in that?"

"I have never been inclined to violence before," he said deliberately, "but since meeting you I have on several occasions been tempted to put you over my knees. You're fool-hardy and idiotic and crazy and stupid and I'm going to kiss you again, Elinor, so don't run away."

I hadn't been going to run away, not before I'd slapped his face. Foolhardy, idiotic, crazy and stupid! But then . . .

He caught my suddenly paralysed hand and smiled faintly. "Yes, you heard right."

"But—"

It was no use, no use at all. I was in love with him.

This time there was no interruption from Egan, no interruption at all. I had the oddest sensation that my bones were melting that I was dissolving in pure liquid joy and then I remembered Madeleine . . .

I pushed him away from me. "Patrick told me tonight that you were going to marry Madeleine. Is it true?"

He didn't answer. He was still holding me but his grip had slackened.

"Is it true?" I cried again.

"Yes. I've asked her to marry me," he said and his grip was now impersonal. He moved to one side. "Come with me. I want to show you something."

"No! I'm not interested." I wrenched away from him and ran to my room. He didn't attempt to follow me but a long time afterwards there was a knock on my door. I didn't answer. I sat there in a frozen silence. I'd locked the door. He couldn't get in.

I saw the handle turn, he called my name, and then he went away.

I was up early the next morning. I hadn't slept much. Chrissie was disturbingly bright and cheerful. She made my head ache and unerringly put her finger on the place that hurt as we went downstairs. Maybe the spot reminded her what Patrick had said. "Is Lee really going to marry Madeleine?"

"Yes." I turned. "Wait for me." I'd not got a handkerchief.

She was standing in front of the old, cracked portrait when I got back. "He looks like Lee, doesn't he?" she said interestedly.

"With good reason," Madeleine said coming up behind us. "Hasn't he told you?"

I knew what was coming. I knew why the portrait had looked familiar. It was Lee. I could see it now.

I listened to Madeleine explaining lightly how Jasper had gone to America, how he had prospered, married and had children, how he had handed down the pride of Winters Hall and how it had gone from father to son through the generations. "Lee came to buy Winters Hall," Madeleine went on. "His father was a rich man, almost a millionaire. When he died Lee thought he would come over to see if he could trace his English relatives. They're like that—Americans. Amusing trait, isn't it?"

"But his name isn't Howard," I said numbly.

"No. His mother was the last of them. She left him all the papers. There was even one from Jasper himself. Barely decipherable of course but it's been authenticated. He urges his son to return to claim Winters Hall and kill the usurpers." Madeleine laughed. "I'm surprised he's not told you. You'd better not let on I've spoiled his secret."

"You said he came to buy it," I said. I felt nothing, only total blankness.

"Oh don't worry. Your father will never sell. We're not that broke." Madeleine caught hold of Chrissie's hand. "Let's eat. I'm starving, aren't you?"

I followed on their heels. "Will you take me into Carsdale, Madeleine? I have to pick up some more clothes."

I couldn't go with Lee, not now.

"Of course," Madeleine said gayly. "Why not?"

There was no one else at the breakfast table. I hoped it would stay that way and I was lucky.

We were on our way soon after half past eight, Chrissie squeezed between us in the little car.

She stayed in it with Madeleine when I went into the house. I didn't want any help.

The door to the den was closed. I didn't open it but went straight upstairs. I filled one of Ken's suitcases with my clothes, packing swiftly.

There was room in the boot for another case. I went back inside and got more of Chrissie's things, a couple of her dolls, her paints and her work basket.

Downstairs the front door slammed.

I went cold all over. I snapped the case shut and rushed out of the room. It must have been the wind.

But it wasn't. It was Mrs. Singer. She leaned against the door, barring the way out for me.

"What do you want?" Fear made my voice shrill.

"I never killed him. I never. He was dead when I got here."

"All right, Mrs. Singer. If you say so." I edged down the stairs, holding the suitcase in front of me like a shield. If she had a knife she was going to have a hard time sticking it through that.

"You don't believe me, do you? It's true. I thought you'd done it."

I stopped. All of a sudden I believed her. "Was Ken expecting you?"

"No. I got to thinking about what you said and I came to have it out with him. I knew they'd blame me, that's why I lit out without saying nothing."

So it *had* been someone from the Hall that Ken had been expecting. I'd been right. "Someone heard me phoning you last night, Mrs. Singer. They're going to tell the police. If I were you I'd get in first."

"Maybe you're right," she muttered. "I nearly went this morning. I was just thinking . . . He had something on me, Nell. I told him some things and he had a little gadget. A kind of tape machine. I wouldn't like the police to find it."

"I don't think it will be here," I said gently. "The police have already looked."

"If you should find it . . . If—"

"I'll destroy it," I promised her. "You weren't the only one he did that to, Mrs. Singer. I'll destroy them all if I get the chance."

"I'm sorry I—I'm sorry I went for you the other day."

"It's all right. I understand."

"I'll go then. I'll go to the police now and tell them."

"Mrs. Singer, did you see anything? A car even?"

She shook her head.

"Did you hear him scream?"

"No. I heard nothing. The door was open. There was a light on in the den, the door there was half open. I went in and there he was."

"All right, Mrs. Singer. Ask for Detective-Inspector Egan. He's a good man."

She opened the door, giving me a weak smile and was gone.

I followed her after a moment and shut the door hard. I'd never have to come back here again.

"So that was Mrs. Singer," Madeleine said as I got back in the car. "Chrissie was getting worried and wanted me to come on in but I knew you would be all right. What did she want?"

"A tape Ken had made. I told her it was no use looking. He'd have hidden it well." I dropped one of the dolls in Chrissie's lap. "Apparently he had a habit of making tapes of conversations he thought might prove to be . . . rewarding."

Madeleine started the car. "A resourceful man," she murmured. "Finished here?"

"Yes." I didn't look back. "Let's go home."

"Home," Madeleine said and she smiled. "To Winters Hall."

"Someone's been messing about with Cindy Lou," Chrissie announced fussing about with her doll. "Her head's all funny."

It was most decidedly askew. I laughed and took her from Chrissie but instead of making things better the head came off in my hand.

"Oh dear!"

"Now see what you've done." She snatched it from me and a scrap of paper fluttered from the hollow body.

I picked it up. A left luggage ticket, hidden away in Chrissie's doll. I knew he'd have picked a good place.

"What is it?" Madeleine asked.

"I think we'd better call at the police station," I said slowly.

She glanced at her watch. "Well, actually I'm in a bit of a hurry and Lee said something about them coming over today. Can't it wait until then?"

"I suppose so."

As if to prove how much of a hurry she was in she put her foot down on the accelerator. I breathed a sigh of relief when we turned in at the Hall. She had proved her driving skill again and again but I preferred a more mundane kind of journey. Chrissie enjoyed it however.

"Would you like to see the secret passage?" Madeleine asked her. "The entrance is near here."

"The real one, you mean?" Chrissie said in delight. "The one that's really a secret?"

"Yes." Madeleine stopped the car and led us across to a small summer house set in a little clearing. Watched with rapt interest by Chrissie she pulled simultaneously on two embossed figures in the stonework and a portion of the wall slid forward. "Come on." She stepped inside, picking up a torch from a ledge.

I was beginning to regret coming. It smelt dank and musty but Chrissie stepped blithely after Madeleine, down some steps and along a narrow tunnel. I had to follow.

The tunnel went in a straight line to the house and there were more steps at the end of it, steep, almost perpendicular, coming out in a little room.

"Exciting, isn't it?" Madeleine put the torch down. "This is over a fireplace. Once the fire was lit no one could get in or out. The fugitive was safe. Let's go down."

There was a trap door opening into the chimney, sooty and dirty. "Watch yourselves," Madeleine said cheerfully. "You didn't see the turret room did you, Elinor? It's just up here. I think I've got time to show you."

More steps, around and around, going higher and higher around a steep well.

"This is the very oldest part of the house," Madeleine said. "All stone as you can see, built to withstand the centuries. But the stairs are not so safe. We nearly had an accident the other day so mother decided this would be out of bounds for the public in future. Careful, Chrissie. Don't go near the edge. It's a long way down." She pushed open a heavy oak door.

The room was round with a tiny barred window. There was no furniture in it.

"Not a very attractive place to spend your last days in. I always felt sorry for the poor lady

275

of the turret. You can make your own way down, can't you? I must rush."

She was gone as she spoke. "I'd like to see out of the window," Chrissie said.

I held her up to it. "There's nothing to see but chimney pots," she said in disgust, "hundreds and hundreds of them."

"Let's go." I didn't like it here. I had no romance in my soul. But when I tried to open the door it wouldn't budge.

Chrissie tugged and pulled with me but it was a fruitless task. "I think it's locked," she said.

"It can't be. It must have jammed."

"It's locked and we can't get out. We'll be up here for ever like the lady in the story." Her face puckered.

I said briskly, "Nonsense! When we don't turn up for lunch, Madeleine will realize what's happened.

"But she made it happen."

"No, it was a mistake." But I didn't sound convincing even to myself. The secret way in, no one seeing us. She could say anything. No one suspected her.

We shouted for a while but it was no use. I knew no one could hear us. I held Chrissie up to the window again and she managed to break the glass, tying my sweater to one of the bars. It was the only way I could think of to attract attention but if the view was over the roof tops I didn't have very much hope of anyone seeing it.

It was cold in that turret room. I tried to talk to keep Chrissie interested but the hours dragged on and we sank into a dull apathy.

When dusk began to fall Chrissie started to cry, "No one's going to come."

"Yes, they will." We were on the floor, huddled close to one another for warmth. I couldn't believe Madeleine would leave us there to slowly starve to death.

But it wasn't Madeleine who came to release us. It was her mother.

We heard the slow creaking of the door as it opened, Mrs. Howard's voice, quivering and tremulous. "Are you there?"

"Yes." I'd have died if that door shut on us again. I hurled myself towards it and grabbed the edge of it.

"She shouldn't have done it." Beryl Howard sounded lost and uncertain. "I wanted you to go—but not like this. Taking a life is wicked." She turned and stumbled down the steps. I caught her arm, afraid she would fall over but she shook my hand off. "Don't touch me. You've ruined us all." She went like quicksilver and by the time Chrissie and I, frozen and stiff, had reached the bottom, she had vanished.

"We'll go to my father," I said.

Chrissie said forlornly, "Can we eat now?"

"Yes. He'll arrange it." I wanted his reassurance, his love, but when we got there the place was empty.

I couldn't believe it. I called his name and went through the rest of the little flat.

Of course he'd have to leave sometime, for some exercise, after dark, when no one could see him.

We went straight down into the kitchen. The cook was there and she gave an almighty shriek when she saw us. "Heavens above! You're safe!"

"Where's my father?"

"Here. I'll get him." She ran out of the kitchen crying excitedly, "They're here. They're safe."

Lee was the first to reach the kitchen, my father making a close second and then the kitchen was full of people, Egan and Turpin, Patrick and Madeleine. The cook hovered and then vanished. There was a babble of voices and then through it all, Chrissie's voice rang childishly accusing. "Madeleine locked us up. In the room where the lady died. We've been there hours and hours."

There was an appalled silence and then Madeleine said reproachfully, "Chrissie! How could you? I wouldn't do such a thing."

"You left us there," I said flatly.

Her rich voice was infinitely sorrowful and pained. "You're trying to get rid of me now, aren't you? You've cooked this up between you, knowing how much your father loves me. You're jealous! And there's Lee too. You want him. I'm in your way." She went up to Lee, burying her face in his chest. "Stop her, Lee. Don't let her do this to me." His arms went round her automatically.

I looked away, at Egan. "I know where Ken hid all his tapes and files," I said. "Will you promise me you'll destroy them when you've got what is relevant? I think that's why Madeleine locked us up. There's probably one of her conversations with Ken."

He nodded and I got the slip of paper out of my pocket and held it out to him.

Before he could take it Patrick had stepped

forward and snatched it out of my hand and then he was running out of the kitchen.

Egan and Turpin were both after him like streaks of greased lightning but I doubted whether they'd catch him. Patrick was younger, fitter and he was on home ground.

"He shouldn't have done that," Madeleine said. "He should have had more faith in me. I'd got nothing to fear from them." She turned around and looked at my father. "You believe me, don't you?"

He hesitated. I didn't blame him. How could anyone believe ill of her?

"You're thinking he'll destroy the ticket," I said tiredly, "but it doesn't make any difference, Madeleine. Now they know where it is, it's merely routine."

If I'd had any doubts then they'd have been dispelled by the look in her eyes. She hated me—more than her mother did—more than Patrick. She said in a low voice, "I didn't want you dead, not at first. I guessed who you were, almost at once. I sent Patrick to make sure. I thought we could block any attempts you made to reach your father but just in case I wanted some ammunition that would prove you were no good. Patrick couldn't find anything, not in your house, not from anyone he talked to. All they said was that you were snooty and stand-offish. Then your stepfather came snooping around, asking questions. I dealt with him easily. He believed everything I said. We came to an agreement. He'd get you a prison sentence. Your father wouldn't want to know you then. Then everything started to go wrong. I didn't want anyone to die. He didn't look such a dangerous man. When he told me what he'd done I almost died myself but then I thought if it came so easily to him he could do it again. I didn't think he'd try blackmail. After all I had more on him. But then I didn't have a record of our conversation."

Egan had come back into the room. She didn't appear to have seen him. Her eyes were fixed on me. "He didn't really leave us any choice. We couldn't endure having him here in the Hall—the money we might have managed. Mother would have helped. But *him* here. And you! No. It was impossible. We went to see him. I thought we could frighten him but he laughed at us. No one laughs at Patrick. He stuck the knife in his stomach. It was horrible. He screamed. And then Patrick killed him. I thought you'd be blamed for it. You should have been. You shouldn't have come here." She buried her face in her hands.

"You'd better come with me," Egan said gently, touching her on the shoulder. "We've got your brother."

"Yes." She went out like a sleepwalker but at the door she turned and looked at Lee. "I really did love you. That didn't help. I saw the way you looked at her. You'll marry her now, won't you? And Jasper will rest in his grave. No more calamities for the Howard family." She smiled and then shrugged and went out with Egan.

No one said anything for quite a while and then Chrissie said in a small voice, "I don't mind if you marry Nell, Lee. I think maybe you'll be too old for me when I grow up."

"Don't talk like that, Chrissie," I said sharply.

"Why not?" my father said. "You love him, don't you." He smiled at me. "For what it's worth you have my blessing."

"Maybe he doesn't like having his life arranged for him so neatly. And maybe all he wants is Winters Hall." I didn't look at Lee but I sensed the silent communication between the two men and then my father said, "Come with me, Chrissie. I think Lee wants to be alone with your sister."

She got up without a word and after a moment Lee said, "You don't believe all I want is the Hall, do you?"

"Why did you ask Madeleine to marry you?"

"She was everything I had always looked for," he said evenly. "Beautiful, charming, intelligent and capable. She would have made the perfect wife. I thought I was lucky and then I met you and you proceeded to turn my world upside down. I didn't want to love you—believe me I fought against it. I didn't want to let Madeleine down."

"Did you suspect her at all?"

"I couldn't."

"But you could suspect me."

"Not really. Will you marry me, Elinor?"

"If it's only to lay the curse I suppose I'd better."

He cupped my face in his hands, his eyes intent. "Is that the only reason?"

"You know it's not."

"I like to be told."

"All right. I love you. I loved you from almost the first moment I saw you."

"Haven't you finished yet?" Chrissie

demanded, putting her head around the door. "Only I'm starving. And all the food is here."

Lee smiled. "We seem destined to be interrupted in one way or another. You'll be hungry too. Wait here. I'll be back in a moment."

My father came in, the cook in tow. His eyes went straight to me and he smiled, satisfied with what he saw. "You'll be happy," he said.

"Are you eating too, Mr. Howard?" the cook asked. "You've hardly had a thing all day."

"I think I will," he said and he sat down at the table.

"You've come out of your world," I said. "It's not so bad, is it? Has anyone fainted?"

He stared at me, taut as a bowstring for a moment, and then he relaxed. "Lee thinks something can be done, even now. In America. I think I'll take a trip."

"We'll come with you," Lee said, coming in with something in his hand. "Your betrothal ring, Elinor."

He unfolded a chamois cloth and the great red ruby of the portrait lay between us. "It will have to be altered," he said, slipping it on my finger. "No one has worn it since Jasper's time."

"The King's charm," my father murmured, his eyes riveted upon it.

I was silent, thinking of the man who had last worn the ring on his finger. Had his hate really been the cause of so much disaster in the Howard family? And would he rest now?

"Don't be afraid," Lee said as if reading my thoughts. "It's all over now."

"Well, can we eat then?" Chrissie said in exasperation.

I laughed and Lee took my hand. I didn't think I would ever be afraid again. I had everything I wanted.

THE END

*Other titles in the
Linford Mystery Library:*

STORM CENTRE
by Douglas Clark
Detective Chief Superintendent Masters, temporarily lecturing in a police staff college, finds there's more to the job than a few weeks' relaxation in a rural setting. He soon gets involved in a local police problem.

THE MANUSCRIPT MURDERS
by Roy Harley Lewis
Antiquarian bookseller Matthew Coll, acquires a rare 16th century manuscript. But when the Dutch professor who had discovered the journal is murdered, Coll begins to doubt its authenticity.

SHARENDEL
by Margaret Carr
Ruth had loved Aunt Cass. She didn't want all that money. And she didn't want Aunt Cass to die. But at Sharendel things looked different. She began to wonder if she had a split personality.

MURDER TO BURN
by Laurie Mantell

Sergeants Steven Arrow and Lance Brendon, of the New Zealand police force, come upon a woman's body floating in the water. When the dead woman is finally identified the police begin to realise that they are investigating a fascinatingly complex fraud.

YOU CAN HELP ME
by Maisie Birmingham

Whilst running the Citizens' Advice Bureau, Kate Weatherley is attacked with no apparent motive. Then the body of one of her clients is found in her room.

DAGGERS DRAWN
by Margaret Carr

Stacey Manston was the kind of girl who could take most things in her stride, but three murders were something different – especially as she had the motive and opportunity to kill them all . . .

THE MONTMARTRE MURDERS
by Richard Grayson

Inspector Gautier of Sûreté investigates the disappearance of artist Théo, the heir to a fortune. Then a shady art dealer is murdered and the plot begins to focus on three paintings by a seemingly obscure artist.

GRIZZLY TRAIL
by Gwen Moffat

Miss Pink, alone in the Rockies, helps in a search for missing hikers, solves two cruel murders and has the most terrifying experience of her life when she meets a grizzly bear!

BLINDMAN'S BLUFF
by Margaret Carr

Kate Deverill had considered suicide. It was one way out—and preferable to being murdered. Better than waiting for the blow to strike, waiting and wondering . . .

BEGOTTEN MURDER
by Martin Carroll

When Susan Phillips joined her aunt on a voyage of 12,000 miles from her home in Melbourne, she little knew their arrival would germinate the seeds of murder planted long ago.

Other titles in the
Linford Western Library:

FARGO: MASSACRE RIVER
by John Benteen

Fargo spurred his horse to the edge of the road. The ambushers up ahead had now blocked the road. Fargo's convoy was a jumble, a perfect target for the insurgents' weapons!

SUNDANCE:
DEATH IN THE LAVA
by John Benteen

The land echoed with the thundering hoofs of Modoc ponies. In minutes they swooped down and captured the wagon train and its cargo of gold. But now the halfbreed they called Sundance was going after it, and he swore nothing would stand in his way.

GUNS OF FURY
by Ernest Haycox

Dane Starr, alias Dan Smith, wanted to close the door on his past and hang up his guns, but people wouldn't let him. Good men wanted him to settle their scores for them. Bad men thought they were faster and itched to prove it. Starr had to keep killing just to stay alive.